THE SCHOOL THAT'S OUT OF THIS WORLD

Hyperspace High is first published in the United States by
Stone Arch Books
A Capstone imprint
1710 Roe Crest Drive
North Mankato, Minnesota 56003
www.capstonepub.com

First published in 2013 by Curious Fox
an imprint of Capstone Global Library Limited,
7 Pilgrim Street, London, EC4V 6LB
Registered company number: 6695582
www.curious-fox.com

Text © Hothouse Fiction Ltd 2013
Series created by Hothouse Fiction
www.hothousefiction.com
The author's moral rights are hereby asserted.

Library of Congress Cataloging-in-Publication Data is available on the
Library of Congress website.
ISBN: 978-1-4342-6307-0 (library binding)
ISBN: 978-1-4342-6311-7 (paperback)

Summary: John learns that museums in outer space are anything but boring
when his class travels to the museum planet of Archivus Major. But the field
trip goes badly wrong when two rival tribes of aliens are accidentally released
from cryogenic storage.

Designer: Alison Thiele

With special thanks to Martin Howard

Printed in the United States of America in Stevens Point, Wisconsin.
042013   007227WZF13

FROZEN ENEMIES

written by ZAC HARRISON • illustrated by DANI GEREMIA

STONE ARCH BOOKS™
a capstone imprint www.capstonepub.com

CHAPTER 1

John Riley was surrounded by aliens. Out of the darkness they came, hundreds and thousands of them: tall gray creatures with large black eyes; little green men; beings with tentacles and antennae, as well as other, even stranger, creatures. Crowding in on him, they babbled in strange languages that John couldn't understand.

Shaking his head, he tried to back away, but the crowd of aliens followed him, pressing closer and closer. One of them reached out with long blue fingers and gripped his shoulder.

"John Riley. *John Riley!* Are you all right? Do you need to go to the medical center?"

John's eyes snapped open. He lifted his head and looked around the room. "W-what . . . huh?" he stuttered. Around him, the aliens had turned in their seats to stare.

It's a dream. I'm dreaming.

His shoulder was shaken again. "John Riley?" said the voice.

John looked up and yelped as he found himself looking into violet eyes with black slits in the center.

Stop freaking out. Calm down. This is not a dream. It's a classroom. You're in a classroom at Hyperspace High.

John blinked for a second. *And you just conked out at your desk*, he was told by a part of his brain that had woken up a little more quickly.

Reality came flooding back.

The alien glaring down at him was the Hyperspace History teacher, Ms. Vartexia. The other aliens were all pupils. And John was a first year at Hyperspace High, the most amazing school in the universe. It had been founded thousands of years ago by the reclusive scholars of Kerallin.

"Uh, Ms. Vartexia," John stammered. "I-I m-must have . . . "

"Fallen asleep," the blue-skinned, bald Elvian finished for him. Taking her hand from his shoulder, she crossed her long, thin arms. Frown lines appeared on her domed forehead.

"Um. I guess I . . . that is . . . well . . . uh . . . " John stuttered.

Nice one, Riley, he told himself silently. *Way to get caught.* Attending school on a vast, technologically advanced spaceship hundreds of light-years from home still felt odd most of the time, but he *was* starting to feel like he belonged here. However odd life on Hyperspace High was, he definitely didn't want to get sent back to a boring Earth school.

The lines on Ms. Vartexia's forehead faded. She looked down a little more kindly. John's shoulders sagged with relief. As he had found out the day he had first arrived at Hyperspace High, the Elvian teacher was strict — and had no sense of humor whatsoever — but she was prone to making mistakes, which meant she was quite forgiving when others messed up.

Good thing it wasn't Doctor Graal's class, John caught himself thinking.

"I shall have to give you some extra work,"

Ms. Vartexia replied briskly. "You are still struggling with Hyperspace History, so you cannot afford to sleep through classes."

John nodded. The punishment could have been a lot worse.

"I also suggest you make sure that you are getting enough sleep," the teacher continued. "I understand Earthlings are a primitive species and require plenty of rest."

Inwardly, John groaned at the word "primitive." In the month he had been at Hyperspace High, he had heard that human beings were a backward species about a thousand times.

But she's right: I'm not getting enough sleep, he told himself.

The previous night, John and his roommate, Kaal, had been exploring the functions of the entertainment ThinScreen in their dorm room after lights out and had discovered a game called *Asteroid Avenger*. They had both become totally engrossed in reaching the final level. A native of the planet Derril, Kaal only needed a few hours' rest each night. By the time John had looked at the clock, it was 2:30 a.m.

Stupid, Riley. That was really stupid, he scolded himself.

"I know that much of what we are learning is new to you," Ms. Vartexia continued, "and I know you are doing well in other subjects. However, I need to see an improvement in your history work. Perhaps another student could help you with your studies?"

John nodded up at the teacher. Once again, Ms. Vartexia was right. He had known nothing about space or alien civilizations throughout the galaxy before one of her mishaps brought him to this school.

Since becoming a Hyperspace High student, he had struggled with every subject except math — but history was easily his worst subject. There was so much to learn. The history of the galaxy stretched back millions of years. Even just studying the most important events meant cramming more knowledge into his brain than he thought it was capable of holding.

While Ms. Vartexia lectured him, John glanced over to a few desks away, where an alien boy with a mane of black hair was sitting. He felt a twinge of envy. Mordant Talliver seemed to absorb lessons without even trying. He always had the best grades in Hyperspace History.

The best grades in almost every class, John reminded himself.

Although Mordant was a bully, John wondered if the half-Gargon boy could help with his own studies.

It might be worth putting up with him if it means I don't get kicked out, John thought.

" . . . So if you wish to pass Hyperspace History this year, I will be looking for much more effort, John Riley."

John's wandering attention snapped back to the teacher. "Yes, thanks, Ms. Vartexia," he babbled. "Sorry I fell asleep. I just stayed up too late last night. It's not because you're boring or anything—"

John heard a snort of laughter. "What a suck-up," Mordant Talliver whispered loudly.

A tennis-ball-sized metal sphere bobbed at Mordant's shoulder, lights blinking across its surface: a Serv-U-Droid called G-Vez that was half servant, half pet.

"Indeed, Master Talliver," the droid said in a snooty voice that sounded ever-so-slightly bored. "The human is obviously trying to escape punishment by using flattery, and as the great Gargon philosopher Huurl once said, 'Flattery is like the burping of Gorpigs.'"

Mordent grinned. "The burping of Gorpigs," he repeated. "Huurl really knew what he was talking about, didn't he?"

"That will do, Mordant Talliver," snapped Ms. Vartexia, turning toward the sneering boy. "If your droid does not stay silent, I will confiscate it."

John rolled his eyes. *What was I thinking?* he asked himself. *Like Mordant would ever help anyone other than himself.*

"Computer," the Elvian teacher said, returning to the front of the class. "End program Vartexia-B-Six-Four-Shard." The screen surrounding the room instantly went blank. "Now, take out your ThinScreens and begin reading about the Goran-Subo war."

As the students rummaged in their bags, John felt a nudge.

"Sorry about that," whispered Emmie Tarz on his right. He watched, dazzled as usual by her beauty, as she flicked silvery hair out of her shining eyes and leaned across her desk toward him. "I did try to wake you up. You were snoring."

"Ha, that wasn't snoring," said a deeper voice from the desk to John's left. "You should try sleeping in the same room as me if you want to hear *real* snoring. It'd make your brain dribble out of your ears."

John turned to look at his roommate. Kaal's leathery wings, green skin, and sharp fangs made him look like some sort of demon.

"It's true," said John with a sudden grin. "Your snoring is probably the reason I didn't get any sleep last night."

"Yeah, right," replied Kaal. "It had nothing to do with playing *Asteroid Avenger* until two-thirty at all."

"Hey," John replied, looking embarrassed. "Just because I can't survive on two hours of sleep . . . "

John's words trailed off, as a flashing orb of colorful light zipped through a solid wall as if it weren't there.

It hovered next to Ms. Vartexia, glittering brilliantly, and then silently changed form in a blaze of light lasting half a second.

Where the ball had been stood a tall alien dressed in white robes. Although he was humanoid in shape, he glowed like a neon light. His head was bald and his face lined with age, but his purple eyes sparkled with humor, making him look youthful.

"Good morning," said Lorem, the

headmaster of Hyperspace High, in a cheerful voice. "I'm sorry to interrupt you, Ms. Vartexia, but I have an important announcement that needs everyone's full attention." He glanced at John, raising one eyebrow.

John bit his lip, blushing.

The headmaster's gaze had already moved on. "Zepp, show the visuals, please."

"Of course, Headmaster," said the voice of the ship's computer, which John had named Zepp — short for Zero-Electronic Personality Pattern — soon after arriving on Hyperspace High. The name had caught on quickly. Now, almost everyone aboard used it.

"Thank you," said the headmaster, as the classroom walls flashed into life again. This time, they showed the surface of a planet. John stared. Across the moving image of the world was a mind-boggling variety of landscapes:

mountains, island jungles, deserts, plains of grass, rivers, lakes, and seas, as well as other vistas that were like nothing John had ever seen.

He saw forests that looked as if they had been built from the insides of an old radio, mountains of lacy steel, temples made of gas, and places so strange that he couldn't begin to guess what they were or what they were made of. Here and there, great stone spires jabbed into the sky, alongside shining glass pyramids, metal domes, spikes of crystal, and buildings that seemed to have been grown rather than built. As scene after scene rolled past, John wondered if the entire planet had been stitched together from a thousand different worlds.

For a few minutes, Lorem allowed the students to watch the strange planet in silence. Then he cleared his throat. "This," he said, "is the museum planet Archivus Major. These images were taken from orbit, as no photography is allowed on the surface. On Archivus Major there are artifacts from every civilization the galaxy has ever known — from atomic artworks to whole landscapes that have been moved across thousands of light years. It is an extraordinary place to visit." The headmaster paused for a moment before finishing, "And in two days' time, myself and Ms. Vartexia will be taking you there."

CHAPTER 2

John couldn't believe it. Archivus Major looked *awesome*. He turned to his two friends and saw that both Emmie's and Kaal's eyes were lit up with excitement.

"Do we *have* to go?" came a voice from John's left.

The headmaster's eyebrow arched again. He stared at the black-haired boy who had spoken. "Most people would consider it an honor just to be allowed to set foot on Archivus Major,

Mordant," Lorem said softly. "Only one group is allowed to visit at a time and the waiting list is years long. You may never have the chance to see its wonders again."

Mordant shrugged. "That's okay, I don't mind," he said. "My grades are perfect in Hyperspace History. I don't need to visit some crumbly old museum."

An edge of steel crept into Lorem's voice. "To answer your question more directly, Mordant: *yes*, you do have to go. Everyone is going. No exceptions."

"But I —"

"Ahh, of course." A look of understanding gleamed in the headmaster's eyes. "It's the Intergalactic Vaporball Championship game in two days' time and — if memory serves — you're a fan, aren't you, Mr. Talliver?"

"I've been waiting for this game all year,"

Mordant said. "The Gargon Bruterippers are playing in the final."

"You can watch the highlights when we return," replied Lorem. It was obvious that as far as he was concerned, the argument was over.

A deep scowl crossed the half-Gargon boy's face, and he crossed his tentacles angrily. The Serv-U-Droid floated at his shoulder. One of its tiny arms extended to flick a microscopic fleck of dust from its master's uniform.

Suddenly, a chiming noise signaled the end of class. As a murmur of excitement ran around the room and students began picking up their bags, Lorem raised his hand for silence.

"Just a few more things," he said. "Firstly, all your normal classes for the next two days have been changed."

A few students cheered.

"Don't get too excited," Lorem said, smiling.

"You'll be doing extra work to catch up." His smile grew wider as the cheers turned to groans. "Secondly, each of you will be traveling to Archivus Major in an individual spaceship — a Xi-Class Privateer, to be exact. It's a ship you won't have piloted before, so Sergeant Jegger will be giving you an intensive course starting in five minutes."

"Wow," John said to Kaal and Emmie, as the headmaster flashed back into the spinning ball of light and sped through the wall. "That woke me up."

"My dad will never believe it," said Kaal, starting toward the door. "He's a history buff and has been trying to get to Archivus Major for years. He's never even made it onto the short list. There are people who've died of old age waiting for their turn."

"It *does* look pretty amazing," Emmie chimed

in as they reached the corridor. "And you know I'm not the greatest fan of Hyperspace History."

"'Pretty amazing' doesn't even begin to cover it," gushed Kaal. "They have the skeleton of an actual Star Dragon — the only one in the universe — plus the original megasculpture of Intergalactic Emperor Gerinim the Vile *and* the ancient golden weapons of the C'perm Sun Tribe *and* —"

"And we really need to get down to the hangar," John cut in. "You know what Jegger's like about being late." Sprinting down the passage, he called ahead, "Hey, Lishtig! Hold that TravelTube for us."

Two minutes later John walked out onto Hyperspace High's main hangar deck. Joining the end of a neat line of students, he stared about him. There were some things about Hyperspace High that he was sure he would never get used to, and the hangar deck was one of them. It was vast. Every time he stepped onto it, he felt like an ant in a football stadium.

Then there were the spaceships.

With a soft click and faint humming sound, the floor in front of the line of students dropped away. Beneath, a new compartment locked into place and the deck rose again. With it came sixteen black, egg-shaped spacecraft, each roughly the size of a large car. *The Xi-Class Privateers,* John guessed.

Standing among the ships was a three-legged alien with a patch over one of his three eyes, a ring of iron-grey hair around his head, and a moustache of the same color.

As the students snapped to attention, Sergeant Jegger ran his gaze down the line, counting. Finding every student had arrived, he gave a grunt of approval and continued. "The

Xi-Class Privateer: it's different from anything you've ever flown before. With eight neutrino-fueled LightFast engines, she's sleek, fast, and powerful. A good ship."

John raised his hand. "Why are we taking individual ships, Sergeant?" he asked. "Why not just go in a shuttle?"

"Headmaster's orders," replied Jegger curtly. "Beyond that, your guess is as good as mine."

"Security's tight on Archivus Major, isn't it?" asked Lishtig, tossing back his purple tail of hair. "Maybe they shoot down any ship that's big enough to carry serious weapons."

"Or maybe it's to prevent the Helvian Mammoths from escaping?" suggested Bareon, huge black eyes blinking in his triangular head.

"More likely so they can tell anyone they don't like the look of to get lost," said the rock-like Gobi-san-Art in his deep, gravelly voice.

"Hey, Mordant, ten credits says you don't last five minutes."

As Mordant began to retort, Sergeant Jegger's voice cut him off. "I thought I was running a flying class down here," he snapped. "Not a gossip session. Shut your flapping mouths and stand by a ship. On the double!"

All the students knew exactly what the sergeant expected of them. In silence, they each made for the nearest Privateer and stood at the nose of the craft. As he approached a ship, John reached out to touch it. Beneath his fingertips the sleek craft felt like ice. John could see circular vents in the Privateer's otherwise smooth shell.

The LightFast engines, he thought.

The other students were murmuring excitedly.

"Settle down," barked Jegger. "I said the Xi-Class Privateer was unlike anything you've flown before and I meant it. Completely different controls to the t-darts you're used to, so I want you to follow my orders very carefully." The sergeant paused, pacing in front of the ships with his odd gait to make sure that everyone was paying attention. Satisfied, he continued. "Each craft has been programmed to respond to its new pilot. Speak your name to open the cockpit. Get in and fasten your safety harness."

"John Riley," said John. A crack instantly appeared in the shell of the ship beside him. Silently, a hatch opened. John stepped in, settling himself into a seat that molded itself around him. A thin harness dropped from above, its straps moving as if they had a life of their own, fitting neatly around his body.

The door slid closed again. "And again: *wow*," John whispered to himself as he looked forward.

From outside, the Xi-Class Privateer had looked like it was made from solid, polished stone. Now, the shell was clear. He had a perfect view of the hangar. Sergeant Jegger stood a few feet away, adjusting his headset.

"All right, cadets. The first thing you'll have noticed is that there's no control panel in front of you." The sergeant's voice sounded in John's cockpit, although he couldn't see any speakers. "The Xi-Class Privateer is piloted using a mixture of voice commands and the controls on the pilot's seat."

John looked down. Sure enough, there were touchpads glowing green at his fingertips.

"Charts, maps, and any other information you need will appear directly on the ship's Formalite skin," Jegger continued. "Try it. Ask for your home planet."

"Earth," said John.

An image of planet Earth appeared in the curved shell, slightly to the right of John's vision. He felt a tiny pang of homesickness. "Set course for Earth?" asked a confident male voice.

"Uh, no. No, thanks," John said quickly.

Further conversation with the Privateer's computer was cut off by Jegger's voice again. "The computer will take care of long-distance navigation, but you'll need to pilot for takeoff and landing and know some basic emergency maneuvers. Speed is at your left hand, direction is at your right hand. . . . "

As the sergeant explained how the craft worked, John listened carefully. He'd become quite good at flying, but his first-ever attempt at piloting a t-dart had been a disaster, as he had ended up crashing into Kaal. Since then, he'd been taking extra lessons and had even saved his classmates' lives by flying an old shuttle off the exploding volcanic planet of Zirion Beta. Learning to fly a completely new type of ship, however, was still nerve-shredding.

"It can take some getting used to, and there's only one way to do that," Jegger told the students. "When I say go, tell your computer to disengage docking locks, start engines, and display speed. Take your craft up slowly and circle the hangar at twenty miles per hour. Tarz. You first. *Go.*"

As John expected, the first ship took off smoothly. Emmie was a natural-born pilot who had an instinctive understanding of flying. For this reason, Jegger often chose her to demonstrate new moves or tactics. Emmie usually showed the rest of the class that whatever Jegger had asked of them wasn't impossible, no matter how difficult.

"Talliver. Go."

The second Privateer took off with a barely

perceptible wobble. John had to admit that Mordant was as talented at flying as he was at everything else, except for making friends.

As he waited for his own turn, John wondered if that was the reason why Mordant's parents had given him G-Vez. No one except the Serv-U-Droid was ever willing to spend more than a few minutes with the half-Gargon.

"Riley. Go."

John's fingertips trembled on the touchpads. Keeping his voice as calm as possible, he said, "Computer, disengage docking locks, start engines, and display speed."

"Affirmative. Ready to launch, John Riley." A large zero appeared in the shell to the left of John's vision.

Following Jegger's advice, and still biting hard on his bottom lip, John moved the index finger of his right hand. The ship rocked backward so that John was looking up to where the other two Privateers were already circling the hangar. He moved his left index finger, and the ship rose into the air. The number zero flickered until it reached thirty-five. John eased off on the speed button.

It wasn't perfect — his trembling fingers meant the Privateer's takeoff was less smooth than Emmie's — but a few seconds later his ship joined the other airborne Privateers.

"Not completely awful," said Jegger. "San-Art. Go."

Once every ship was zooming around the ceiling of the hangar, the sergeant began giving instructions for maneuvers.

Before long, the egg-shaped ships were swooping around the hangar as the students' confidence increased.

Jegger kept up a constant stream of

comments: "Werril, you can go a little faster than *that*, cadet. What are you: a little old Wussian with some heavy shopping? Temerate, make your ship lean into the turns. Talliver, *stop showing off*!"

The last comment had barely registered when Mordant's Privateer suddenly sped dangerously close to John's. Mordant's face leered at John for a moment, then his ship accelerated away to the far end of the hangar. Shaken, John's fingers slipped on the touchpad, sending his own Privateer spiraling off wildly.

Seething with anger, John brought his ship back under control. For a second he caught himself wishing desperately that the Privateer had weapons that he could use to shoot down the half-Gargon. Fighting down the urge to give chase, and cursing under his breath, John returned to flying up and down the hangar, concentrating instead on getting used to the Privateer's controls.

"Lishtig ar Steero!" Jegger shouted. "Why are you flying upside down? For goodness' sake, boy, stop. That's good — now use the right-hand control pad . . . the *right* . . . to flip. No, not *all* the way around, now you're upside down again —"

As Jegger tried to right Lishtig's ship, John executed a neat turn and zoomed off down the hangar again. He frowned. Mordant Talliver was once again heading directly toward him. John touched the control pad to swerve away. His mouth fell open as Talliver's ship mirrored the move. With Jegger's attention elsewhere, Mordant was playing chicken with him.

Desperately, John moved his fingers on the unfamiliar control pads, trying to get out of the way. His Privateer turned, skimming inches past

Mordant's ship just in time to avoid a crash. From the corner of his eye, John saw Mordant grinning and making a rude gesture with his tentacles. Suddenly, Emmie's ship was right in front of his own. Mordant had forced him to fly straight into her!

For a split second, John saw Emmie staring at him, mouth moving in a shout of warning, eyes wide in shock.

"Riley. *Riley*. What in Trud's name are you doing?" yelled Jegger, as John's ship smashed into Emmie's, then tumbled toward the deck.

Emmie recovered quickly; her ship flew off unharmed. John struggled to regain control, but the fall was too quick. His ship smacked into the deck like a dropped stone, bounced, and rolled into a corner of the hangar. Although the Privateer's seat and safety harness softened the landing, John felt like he was in a washing machine. But worse was the shame, as he realized that once again he'd crashed a ship on Jegger's deck. Closing his eyes, he let out a loud groan.

By the time he opened his eyes again, Emmie and Kaal's Privateers hovered a few yards away. His friends peered down at him, concern on their faces.

Jegger was still bellowing into his headset. "Riley, report. Report *now*! Are you all right, boy? If you've damaged that ship, I'll have you scrubbing the entire deck with a toothbrush."

"Sorry, sir," John replied at last, his voice shaking with shock and anger. Knowing that if he told the truth, it would look like he was trying to shift the blame, he continued, "I must have been going too fast."

"Do you *think* so, Riley?" Jegger shouted, stomping across the deck on his three legs. His face was bright red and his mustache bristling. "I thought you were shaping up to be a good pilot, but it turns out you're just a speed demon looking for thrills. Well, not in my ships, Riley. And not on my hangar deck."

The tongue-lashing lasted several minutes, by which time the whole class had lowered their Privateers. Cheeks burning, John tried not to look at Mordant, wearing a grin so wide, it looked like the top of his head might flip off.

Eventually, the sergeant calmed down enough to give orders again. "Line up," he told the class. "As some of you obviously want to crash every single one of my ships, the rest of the class will be devoted to emergency landings," he croaked, voice ragged from shouting.

"Safety Code Violation."

Every head swung around.

At the far end of the hangar a hovering shape

was framed in the doorway of the TravelTube. Completely white, it looked like a white ball on top of a larger egg. Blank-faced, and with no trace of emotion in its electronic voice, the Examiner somehow managed to seem threatening. Even Sergeant Jegger was silent as the machine floated forward.

"John Riley," the Examiner continued, making itself heard inside every Privateer, "you have failed to acquire the minimum flight competency required for the Archivus Major field trip."

John gulped.

"Your status is under review. Failure will result in the cancellation of your participation."

"Um . . . what?" John asked, still shaken by his crash and not following what the white machine was telling him.

"You crashed, John Riley. Now you must be examined," the machine said, floating back toward the TravelTube. "On the morning of the trip to Archivus Major your flight skills will be tested. If you fail, you will be kept behind."

CHAPTER 3

Sprawled across a deep, black sofa in the dorm
room he shared with Kaal, John stared moodily
at a large entertainment ThinScreen. He was
trying to watch a Sillaran show called *Black
Star 360*, but he couldn't understand the plot.
It involved a Sillaran woman dressed in black,
flying around the galaxy trying to find the Holy
Chalice of P'rawn and killing lots of aliens
along the way. Why she was looking for the

chalice and what the aliens had done to upset her wasn't explained.

No matter how hard John tried to concentrate, his thoughts kept returning to his earlier crash.

The Examiners were notoriously harsh. It wouldn't be easy to get through any test they had created. Now, John was convinced that he'd messed up his chances of seeing the museum planet.

With a sigh, he looked around his room for something to take his mind off the problem. Outside the floor-to-ceiling viewing window, stars streamed by as Hyperspace High powered its way through the galaxy. It was a sight of incredible beauty, but John's gaze moved onto the long desk against the opposite wall.

There, two ThinScreens were currently switched off.

He thought about getting started on the extra work that Ms. Vartexia had given him, but he decided he wasn't in the mood.

Next to the desk was a door to the bathroom, which contained a jet bath the size of a small swimming pool.

No. If I take a bath, I'll get into my pajamas, and it's way too early for that, John thought, feeling sorry for himself.

His gaze rested on his bed pod. There was one at either end of the room. The pods also had food and drink portals and another entertainment ThinScreen that John used when he didn't want to disturb Kaal.

Remembering the twinge of homesickness he had felt when the Privateer showed him an image of Earth, John made a decision.

"I'll call Mom and Dad," he said to empty air. "That will cheer me up."

"Will you be wanting to make a Skype call?" asked a deep, friendly-sounding voice.

"Oh, hi, Zepp. Yeah, that would be great. Could you please set it up?"

"As always, it will be a pleasure," replied the computer. "But you know the rules. You'll have to change your clothes."

"Sure." John crossed to his locker and pressed a hand to the pad that opened it. Pulling off the red and silver Hyperspace High uniform he was wearing, he picked out a plain white T-shirt and jeans.

When Lorem had invited him to remain on the ship as a student, he had made it clear that John's parents could never know that he wasn't where he was supposed to be — at a boarding school called Wortham Court in Derbyshire.

"Ready." John sat cross-legged on his bed and checked behind him to make sure that nothing would be visible to his parents except a plain white wall.

The ThinScreen flicked on, showing the Skype homepage. Zepp had already patched into Earth's internet, hundreds of light years away, and placed the call.

A few moments later his mother answered, looking flustered but pleased to see him. "John," she said, smoothing her tousled hair. "Sorry, I just came in from working in the garden. Windy out, isn't it?"

"Hi, Mom. Great to see you. How was your day?" John smiled at the screen and carefully changed the subject.

It could have been raining goats over his parents' house, for all he knew about the weather on Earth.

"Garbage!" his father interrupted, leaning over his wife's shoulder. "The wind blew the cans over. There's garbage all over the garden. How was yours?"

"Oh, the usual," replied John, already feeling happier. It didn't matter what they said, the sight of his parents' faces always cheered him up. "I'm not doing that well in history, but the teacher's okay. She and the headmaster are taking us to a museum in a couple of days."

"Oh, I didn't know there were any history museums near your school," his father replied. "Where is it?"

"Um . . . uh . . . " John choked, unable to answer.

A message flashed up on the screen.

"The History of the World Museum," John said with relief, thanking his stars that Zepp was able to help. "It's kind of a long drive, but we're taking off early."

"Well, I hope it helps you with your grades,"

said his mother. "You look tired. There are black circles under your eyes. Are you getting enough rest?"

John rubbed his eyes. "I did stay up too late last night, I guess," he admitted sheepishly.

"Make sure you get an early night tonight," said his mom, sounding concerned. "You don't want me to write to the headmaster, do you?"

"Ugh, no, Mom. I definitely don't want that."

"Leave the boy alone," his dad added, grinning. "He's probably been having midnight feasts with his friends, or whatever it is they do at fancy boarding schools. Isn't that right, son?"

"Uh, yeah. Sort of, Dad."

"So, apart from goofing off in the middle of the night, what else have you been up to?" Dad asked.

John didn't enjoy lying to his parents, but he

knew it was necessary. If he didn't give them some fake details about his life at Wortham Court, they might become suspicious. Nevertheless, he tried to keep his stories as close to the truth as possible.

"Just hanging out with my friends Carl and Emma," he told them. "We study together in the library, and Carl's been teaching me martial arts."

As he chatted with his mom and dad, John slowly relaxed. The question about the museum had been a close call, but after a month on Hyperspace High, he was getting used to telling his parents what they expected to hear. Without ever mentioning that "Carl" and "Emma" were from different planets, he had told them everything about his friends. In his tales, Zepp was a computer whiz who loved music, while Lorem was Professor Holt, the learned headmaster who seemed to know everything. Hyperspace High itself became the converted stately home John had seen in the brochures about Wortham Court.

He only realized that he had become a little too relaxed when he found himself saying, "And I made a fool of myself in a flying lesson —"

As the words left his mouth, he knew he had made a mistake. His mom and dad were blinking in surprise.

"*Flying lesson!*" his dad yelped. "Wortham Court gives you *flying* lessons?"

"Surely they don't let students pilot aircraft," his mother said, looking pale.

"Yeah . . . um . . . no . . . uh," John stammered. He stared at the screen, hoping that Zepp could come up with some way he could explain the flying lessons.

Nothing.

He was on his own.

Panicking, John gabbled the first thing that came into his head. "It must be a bad connection. I said 'frying' lesson. The school gives us cooking lessons. You know, the importance of nutritious food and all that. We call them 'frying lessons.' Anyway, I dropped an apple pie I'd made into someone's bag. Made a complete mess of all their work . . ."

John took a deep breath, watching his parents' faces closely.

His dad was first to speak. "*You* are learning how to cook?"

"Oh, yeah. It's fun," John said, nodding furiously. "Cake and, uh, soup, and all that."

"But you've never even been able to boil an egg," his mom cut in.

John shrugged. "Well, I wouldn't say I'm a top chef yet, but I'm learning."

"Great. You can make Christmas dinner this year," his dad said, grinning.

John's shoulders sagged. He was glad that his parents had swallowed the story, but at the same time, he felt ashamed for telling them such an enormous lie.

Forcing a smile onto his face, he ended the call as quickly as he could. He couldn't face the thought of having to come up with any more lies that night.

"Phew. Sorry, Zepp. That was really close," he said, taking a deep breath when the screen had gone blank.

"Your parents believed you," replied the computer calmly. "Are you all right?"

The call over, John's worry about the flying examination came flooding back. With another sigh, he leaned against the wall. Over the past month, he had come to share his innermost thoughts with the computer. Zepp was always cheerful, often made him laugh, and usually had something helpful to say.

"I'm worried about having to take this test for the Examiners," John admitted. "If I fail, I'll be stuck here while everyone else goes to Archivus Major. I thought I was getting good at flying, but that's my second crash. I messed up in Hyperspace History today, and I can't even get my story straight for my parents. I don't want to leave Hyperspace High, but at this rate Lorem is going to think letting me stay was a mistake."

"That is unlikely," said Zepp's voice gently. "Accessing your report file, I see that Sergeant Jegger has made positive comments about your flying abilities, and many other teachers say that you are trying hard in subjects that are completely new to you. Professor Dibali thinks that one day you could become one of the school's leading mathematicians. The general opinion among the staff is that you have the potential to be an excellent student. As I have mentioned before, the headmaster rarely makes mistakes."

"But —" John began.

"Perhaps if you had a little more faith in yourself, things wouldn't seem so bad. Of course, it would help if you made sure the inefficient lump of goo you call a brain always had enough sleep."

John grinned. He couldn't hide anything from the computer.

"I might add that no problem was ever solved by sitting around feeling sorry for yourself," Zepp added. "Why don't you take a night off, have some fun, and get to bed on time?"

"Thanks, Zepp. Has anyone ever told you that you're a good friend?"

"No. No, they haven't," replied the computer, sounding taken aback and pleased at the same time.

"Well, it's true."

Just then, the dormitory door hissed open.

"John!" yelled Kaal, running into the room, his wings flapping in excitement. "You've got to come, now."

"What?" John scrambled to the edge of his bed pod. "What's the matter?"

"Nothing's the matter," said Emmie Tarz, walking in calmly behind the big Derrilian. "He's just really excited. There's a special showing at the 4-D movie theater. It starts in five minutes."

"Vartexia arranged it," Kaal said. "One of Archivus Major's most famous exhibits is a frozen battle between the Goran and the Subo, so she asked the theater to show *Battleground*

Zero. It's a classic. Come on, hurry up, what are you waiting for?"

"Hang on, what's a 4-D theater?" John asked.

Emmie and Kaal stopped and looked at each other. "He's never seen a 4-D movie, Kaal," said Emmie, with mock seriousness. "I don't suppose they have them on Earth."

"Well, Emmie, then it's our duty to make sure he does," replied Kaal. "You grab his right arm, I'll take the left."

Laughing, the two of them hauled John out of his bed pod. John allowed himself to be hustled through the door, joining in their laughter.

Zepp's right, he thought. *No point in worrying all night.*

* * *

"So what happens now?" John whispered.

They were sitting in a dark, cave-like room. About sixty students sat waiting in MorphSeats, which molded to the shapes of their bodies in the same way that the seats in the Xi-Class Privateers did.

"Wait and see. Here, do you want some Walja Tots for the movie?" Kaal replied, passing John a bag.

Excitedly waiting for the 4-D film, John had temporarily forgotten how revolting Kaal's food looked in the cafeteria every day. Without thinking, he popped a Walja Tot into his mouth.

"Ugh, Kaal, this is disgusting. This thing tastes like fishy blue cheese," he said, trying not to gag.

"How can you not like Walja Tots? They're delicious."

The student in front of them turned his

head. He looked like a white bat. "Shhhh," he hissed. "The movie's starting."

Dim lights went out. In the darkness, John felt like he was floating in space. He blinked in astonishment as he realized he *was* floating in space.

All around him, above and below, stars twinkled. A comet flashed past, so close he could almost reach out and touch it. Planets whirled around him. The temperature in the room had dropped to freezing, and the gravity was gone. John felt goosebumps crawling up his arms as he floated free of his seat, slowly turning in the depths of space.

"W-w-wow," he croaked.

"*Shhhh.*"

A deep voice boomed in the silence. "For every species there comes a time when it takes its first footsteps into the unknown darkness beyond the stars." The voice paused for a moment and a star lit up. John felt like he was hurtling through space as it became bigger and bigger, before seeing planets spinning around the star.

"One sun, two planets," the voice continued. "Suboran, belonging to the Subo, a species with a history of bloodshed and battle. Gora Prime, belonging to the proud and independent Goran. When the Subo discovered the secrets of space travel, they turned upon the neighboring planet and started a violent war that raged out of control. . . . "

The scene changed. Now John found himself sitting on a rock by the edge of a sea. Gravity had returned, and the MorphSeat had become hard with sharp edges. A salty wind blew across the scene, tangling John's hair.

" . . . A WAR THAT ALMOST

DESTROYED THE GALAXY!" boomed the voice. Instantly, there was a heavy rumbling. The rocks shook and strange, four-winged birds took to the sky, crying in terror.

John turned his head. Over the crest of a craggy hill, an oddly shaped, bright-red tank appeared. It stopped for a second, then crashed down the rocks toward him.

"Will you be *quiet!*" snapped the bat-like student in front. John hadn't realized that he'd yelped in shock. "Haven't you ever seen a 4-D movie before?"

John was unable to take his eyes off the tank thing. Now he realized that it wasn't on wheels but on dozens of short, heavily armored legs. Great crab-like pincers jutted from its body. As it ran past, he could smell it.

He realized that it wasn't a machine at all. It was an alien creature.

Just as the alien was about to crush the audience beneath its weight, it changed course. A hole opened in its crusty armor. In a voice like a whirlwind, it bellowed, "FOR GORA PRIME!" and crashed into the sea. A huge wave rolled up the rocks. John gasped as cold water hit him.

"Into the sea. The Goran spy escaped into the water!"

John spun around as the booming voice shouted behind him. Dozens of massive, seal-like creatures had appeared on the craggy rocks around him. Small, dark eyes flashed in their gray faces. Their blubbery bodies moved forward on grasping limbs that ended in webbed claws. Each one had a sharp metal spike jutting out of its forehead. These, John guessed, must be the Subo.

"After it, you cowards! Quickly," roared one

of the seal creatures, exposing its terrifying teeth and long, hideous tongue. "I want it dead. A reward for the Subo who kills it."

"Yes, General Klort!" shouted what John assumed must be Subo soldiers. Waddling forward with surprising speed, they splashed into the ocean, soaking John once more.

The scene changed again and again, as the story of the brave Goran spy battling through enemy lines to carry Subo battle plans back to Gora Prime unfolded.

John barely knew where to look. The movie was so real, it was as if he was experiencing the action himself, sometimes soaked to the skin in icy waters and sometimes burned by a desert sun.

As the final battle reached its peak, he could no longer contain his excitement.

Risking another shushing, he whispered,

"This is so freaking amazing," in Kaal's direction.

"Yeah," Kaal replied. "They do it with HoloProjectors, Nerve Stimulators, and Sense Enhancers. You're not actually wet; your body just thinks . . . "

"*Gahhhhh!*" John's shout cut off Kaal midsentence. The Goran had been about to board its ship, when a monster leaped from the sandy ground where it had been hiding. The floor rumbled beneath John's feet.

He recognized the long, gray form of General Klort as it twisted in the air and bellowed a war cry. As it turned, the long, sharp laser-horn protruding from the general's bulbous head plunged straight for John's heart. Unable to stop himself, he lurched back blindly to avoid the point, flailing his arms and falling from his MorphSeat in sheer terror.

"Stupid first year. You totally ruined the end of the movie."

John opened his eyes to see the bat-student glaring at him.

When he heard a giggle, he looked up. His head was in Emmie's lap. She grinned down at him, her eyes glistening with amusement.

"Did you enjoy the movie, Earthling?" she said, laughing, patting him on the forehead.

Still shaking with shock, John staggered to his feet as the lights came on. "That was *awesome*," he whispered. "Thank goodness it was just a movie. I'd hate to get into a fight with one of those Subo things for real."

CHAPTER 4

Just as Zepp had predicted, John felt more positive after a good night's sleep. The breakfast that appeared from the food dispenser at his table in the cafeteria also helped: ice-cold orange juice and a fruit salad, followed by scrambled eggs and toast.

By the time he took a place between Kaal and Emmie on a MorphSeat in lecture hall A, he was beginning to think he might actually get to Archivus Major. After all, as Emmie had pointed out over breakfast, he was shaping up to be a good pilot. If Mordant Talliver hadn't caused the crash the day before, he would have flown the Privateer as well as anyone in the class.

Laying his ThinScreen on the small desk in front of him, John looked down toward the lecturer. A short being with an enormous, blotchy head stood talking to the headmaster. John's first impression was that the new arrival looked nervous. His hands moved constantly, patting his head and loose robes as if to check that they were still there. John shrugged and turned his attention elsewhere. He was getting used to seeing the aliens of many different worlds and knew the twitchy movements might be completely normal for the small being.

With only one day to go before the field trip, excitement was running high. Many of the students had been reading about the exhibits on the museum planet, and each one wanted to see something different.

"I'm going to the tomb treasures of Gormib the Reaper," said Bareon, a few seats down from John.

"Sheesh, who wants to look at a pile of old jewels," cut in Queelin Temerate. "I want to see the space galleon *Corsair*."

"No way, it's got to be the Star Dragon," Kaal insisted.

Only Mordant looked less than pleased, John noticed as he looked around. The half-Gargon was leaning back in his chair, tentacles behind his head and a scowl on his face. G-Vez bobbed about him, lights flashing. John couldn't hear what it was saying, but whatever it was made Mordant's scowl deepen.

"A very good morning to you all," said Lorem, stepping forward and addressing the students with his usual cheer. As the room fell silent, he continued. "It is my great honor to present to you Graximus Greyfore, the head curator of Archivus Major and the only living resident on the planet. He will be giving you some very important information this morning, so please listen carefully."

Stepping back, the headmaster gave the being a small bow.

Graximus Greyfore coughed. "Ahh . . . y-yes . . . w-well now . . . " he stammered in a high, squeaky voice, before stopping to cough again. "G-g-good morning."

The curator seemed to realize he wasn't making a good impression and took a deep breath. "As your headmaster says, I am G-Graximus Greyfore . . . yes, Graximus Greyfore," he continued, sounding only very slightly more confident. "I am here to instruct you on how to b-behave on Archivus Major. First, you must not touch anything. . . . "

"Perhaps you might start by telling the students why these rules are so important," Lorem interrupted gently.

"A-ahh, yes. Of course," Greyfore stuttered. "Th-the rules are not only to make s-sure that our exhibits are not damaged, but also to ensure your own s-safety. Most of our artifacts are ancient and very d-delicate. Many are extremely d-dangerous. One touch in the w-wrong place could have disastrous consequences. H-hideously mangled bodies, killer viruses released, destruction raining down . . . "

At last, Greyfore began warming to his audience. John listened with rapt attention, as the large-headed curator listed the terrors that might be unleashed on Archivus Major.

"I think they get the message," said Lorem

firmly, as Greyfore began detailing some of the more horrific ancient weapons displayed on the planet.

"Security is extremely t-tight on Archivus Major," Greyfore continued, changing tack. "As y-your headmaster s-said, I am the only l-l-living being on the p-planet, but I frequently t-t-travel to acquire new collections. I w-w-will not be there when you v-visit, but everything is c-completely automated to p-prevent contamination. No one lands without pre-approval, and all approaching visitors are DNA ch-checked. Once on the planet, you will find a force of Omega-bots, whose job it is to p-protect the exhibits. They will not h-h-hesitate to remove you from the planet if the rules are breached. Rule one: you must not t-touch anything unless given permission to do so. Rule t-two: the Omega-bots must be obeyed at all times. Rule three . . . "

For the next hour, the strange curator outlined the planet's rules. There were hundreds. Despite having had a full night's sleep, Greyfore's speech was beginning to make John feel drowsy. Finally, he said, "As you can see, we take s-s-security very seriously. S-so, it is crucial that you remain alert at all t-times."

"Thank you, Graximus," said Lorem. "Perhaps you'd be so kind as to take some questions from the students?"

The curator nodded his enormous head. "Certainly, H-h-headmaster. And b-b-before I forget, for security reasons, I will need to see the Galactic Fleet Holo-registrations for all the ships t-t-traveling to Archivus Major."

"Of course," Lorem said. "I will just have a word with Sergeant Jegger. Students, I'm sure you will show our guest every courtesy while I step out."

The curator's eyes followed Lorem, as the headmaster flashed into a ball of energy and sped away. Then Greyfore turned back to the students.

"Before I take your questions, perhaps you would allow me to ask a few of my own."

John looked up, surprised at the small curator's change of tone. He shrugged. Perhaps the headmaster had made him nervous, or perhaps he was more comfortable now that his speech on Archivus Major was finished.

"First, is there anyone here who likes vaporball?"

Several students looked at each other. "Weird question for the curator of Archivus Major to ask," John whispered to Kaal.

"Maybe he's a bit, you know, *eccentric*," Kaal replied. "He *does* live on that planet all by himself."

Mordant Talliver's tentacle was up in the air in a flash. "I love vaporball," he said.

"Excellent," said Greyfore with a chuckle, stepping down from the podium and walking over to where Mordant was sitting. Taking a hand out of his pocket, he placed it on the half-Gargon's shoulder. "I'm sure you know the Intergalactic Vaporball Championship is being held on Plarz."

"Yes, I know that," replied Talliver.

"Plarz is only a few light-years away from Archivus Major. You'd like to go there instead of Archivus Major, wouldn't you?" Greyfore said intensely, staring straight into Talliver's eyes — any trace of his stutter had disappeared.

"Yes, I would like to go to Plarz."

To John, Mordant's voice suddenly sounded strangely flat.

He glanced at Kaal, but the Derrilian was

making notes on his ThinScreen and didn't seem to have noticed.

The curator removed his hand from Mordant's shoulder. "Such a shame you'll be visiting our exhibits instead," he chuckled. "Now, who would like to earn extra credit?" he asked, reaching into his robes and pulling a small device from his pocket.

Emmie's hand was in the air instantly. "Extra credit," John heard her whisper. "If anyone needs *that* around here, it's me."

Me too, John thought, wishing he'd been quick enough to get his hand in the air first. However, Graximus Greyfore was already standing next to Emmie, one hand on her shoulder, the other showing her the device.

"As you know, photography has never been allowed on Archivus Major," he said, looking around the class. "However, we have just developed a device that will capture 4-D images without interfering with any artifacts." Holding up the small black cube, he continued. "We call it the Comet Creative. This student will be the first to photograph our exhibits. The images she takes will be the first ever taken on the planet's surface."

Greyfore paused for a moment and stared deeply into Emmie's eyes. "This prototype will only take a few pictures. Make sure you only photograph the Goran-Subo battleground. It's our most famous exhibit. People will want to see it first. Have you got that?"

"I will only photograph the Goran-Subo battleground," Emmie promised in a flat voice, taking the Comet Creative.

"Let's keep it a secret for now," the curator said with a chuckle. He patted Emmie's shoulder and looked around at the other students. "Imagine how surprised and proud your headmaster will be when he finds out your classmate's images will be seen by the whole galaxy."

"Yeah, right," sneered Mordant. "Emmie Tarz is as dumb as a box of Lorpsnails. You'll probably get two hundred pictures of the inside of her pocket."

"Very clever, Master Talliver," G-Vez said in its haughty voice. "Huurl himself would be dazzled by your sharp wit."

John ignored the small machine. "Shut your mouth, Mordant," he snapped, fingers curling into fists. "At least she's not —"

"Please, please," said Greyfore, holding up a hand for silence. "Thank you, Ms. . . . ahh . . . Tarz, is it?"

Emmie nodded.

"I'm sure you'll do very well," the curator

said, smiling as he made his way back to the podium. "Ahh, H-headmaster," he said, as the door opened and Lorem entered with Ms. Vartexia.

Lorem was holding the Holo-registrations. "Forgive me for taking so long, Graximus, but I wanted to introduce my travel companion for this excursion. May I present Ms. Vartexia."

The curator bowed to the Elvian instructor, then looked over the glowing registration certifications.

"G-g-good, good," Greyfore said, nodding his head. "Everything looks to be in order." John noticed that the curator's voice sounded high and squeaky again, and his stutter had returned. "Now, I've an urgent m-meeting with our artifact c-collectors on Crigon, but I d-do have time for one or t-two more questions."

Kaal's hand was the first up.

"Y-yes," Greyfore stuttered. "What would you l-like to know about Archivus M-major?"

"What is the Goran-Subo battleground?" Kaal asked.

"Ahh, our most famous exhibit," Graximus Greyfore said, nodding again. "It is the last battle of the Goran-Subo war. The longest, most glorious war in galactic history. A war that lasted a thousand years."

"And threatened the extinction of hundreds of species," Lorem murmured, loud enough for the class to hear.

"When you say it's the last battle, do you mean it's, like, a full-scale replica?" Bareon cut in.

"No, I mean it's the actual battle," replied Greyfore gravely. "The magnificent Subo Army was on the verge of finally crushing the Goran once and for all —"

"Actually, the two armies were evenly matched." Ms. Vartexia cut in.

Greyfore glanced at the Hyperspace History teacher. "The Goran line was about to be shattered by a Subo attack —" he continued.

"An attack led by the most ruthless general in the Subo Army," Ms. Vartexia interrupted again.

For a moment, Greyfore looked like he might explode. With obvious effort, he collected himself. "General Klort was a hero," he said curtly.

"She lost every battle she was involved in," Ms. Vartexia said.

Anger again flashed in Greyfore's eyes, then he flapped his hands as if waving away Ms. Vartexia's words.

"As I was saying," he growled, "a galactic peacekeeping force arrived at the climax of the battle. Using advanced technology, it froze the entire battlefield. All of the soldiers have since been kept in one huge stasis cube exactly as they were at that time. We will never know how the battle would have ended."

"However, the Subo and Goran have lived in peace on their neighboring planets ever since," said Lorem lightly.

"Indeed," said Greyfore, in a voice that was almost a bark. "Now, I am s-sorry but I really must leave if I am to b-be on time f-for my m-meeting."

"Well, I'm sure I speak for all the students when I thank you for your visit," replied Lorem politely.

"Of course. I-it's always good to m-meet interested young historians," Greyfore said. "I hope you all have an e-excellent visit to Archivus M-major."

Glancing up at Ms. Vartexia, he added, "An Elvian, eh?" He reached out and touched Ms. Vartexia on the arm, staring up into the tall teacher's eyes. "You *must* try the Elvian spaghetti at Optical Orbit in the evening. It's *very* good. You will want to keep eating it all night."

"Excuse me, sir," said Lishtig, thrusting one of his hands into the air. "Are we staying *overnight?*"

"Well, of course we're staying overnight," said the headmaster, as Graximus Greyfore hurried out of the lecture hall. "There's far too much to see in a single day. I thought you would have guessed. That's why you will each be taking a Xi-Class Privateer. Every ship will double as a bed pod."

Despite Graximus Greyfore's strange behavior and all the curator's rules, the trip was sounding like more and more fun.

Gritting his teeth, John reminded himself that first he had to pass the Examiners' test.

CHAPTER 5

Billows of steam rolled around the bathroom, as John soaked under a soapy spray. "What's the time, Zepp?" he shouted over noisy jets of water that gushed from all directions.

"It is now five zero three and thirty-two seconds," the computer replied. "You should think about getting dressed."

"Okay, but could you turn the temperature down? A few seconds of cold should wake me up."

"*Yeeeow!*" John yelled a second later. "Not that cold! Turn it off. Turn it *OFF*!"

"Awake now?" Zepp seemed to chuckle as the water cut off and whirring fans began blasting John with warm air.

"For a bunch of old wires and circuit boards, you have a real cruel streak. You know that, don't you?" John complained, as he stepped out of the shower cubicle, completely dry but still shivering.

"Yes," said the computer. "This might help you wake up, too." Loud Earth rock music began playing.

John brushed his teeth, trying to keep his nerves under control. In a few minutes he would have to face the Examiners.

In his mind he went over everything that Sergeant Jegger had taught about flying the Xi-Class Privateer over the past two days. "Speed on the left, direction on the right," he muttered to himself through a mouthful of foaming toothpaste.

Zepp startled him. "Message from the Examiners. Report immediately to hangar C for your flight test. Good luck."

"Thanks," John said. He pulled on his uniform. Then he headed out of the room. He got as far as the door before remembering to return to the sink to spit, rinse, and return the toothbrush to its holder.

Kaal's head emerged from his bed pod just as John was leaving.

"Don't forget," he said, yawning, "we're meeting at the Center for a celebration breakfast after you've passed."

"*If* I pass."

"You'll pass," said Kaal, as the door hissed shut.

* * *

"Proceed," droned the Examiner.

"Uh, John Riley," said John, his voice shaking.

A hatch opened in the side of the sleek, black spaceship. John sat in the pilot's MorphSeat, and the harness strapped itself around his body.

One tiny mistake and I'll be left behind. . . .

He didn't finish the thought. Instead, he scolded himself, remembering Zepp's advice. "Get a grip. I *am* good at this. Even Jegger said so," he said out loud.

Feeling slightly more confident, he placed his hands on the armrests of the seat, setting his fingertips directly on the touchpad controls. Through the ship's transparent shell, he looked toward the single Examiner floating close by, and nodded.

"Computer, disengage docking locks, start engines, and display speed," he said, pushing down another wave of anxiety.

"Affirmative. Ready to launch, John Riley."

From the corner of his eye, John saw red lights flash on the blank whiteness of the Examiner's "head." Its voice broke in through the Privateer's intercom. "Maneuvers. First: circle the deck and make a rotating ninety-degree turn, taking a new stationary position at the hangar bay doors."

John gulped. As he'd expected, the Examiner wasn't going to make it easy for him. "Computer: display course heading," he said. New information flashed up on the transparent skin of the Privateer. John's fingers were already moving across the touchpads.

He had barely finished the first maneuver when the Examiner issued new commands. One after another, John completed them flawlessly, his confidence growing steadily each time.

In the back of his mind, he wished Emmie was watching. *This must be how she feels when she's flying*, he thought.

As he took the Privateer around the hangar in a series of turns, rolls, and swoops, he felt — for the first time — like he was a part of the ship.

"Land and exit Xi-Class Privateer," said the Examiner at last. Its voice gave no clue as to whether it was satisfied or not.

"Okay, Riley, last one. Don't mess this up," John whispered through gritted teeth, as he brought the spaceship around and lined up for landing. "Computer, display docking guides," he said.

Carefully, he brought the ship onto the deck. The Privateer landed smoothly.

Upon landing, the harness released, and John stumbled out on legs like jelly. He stood at attention in front of the Examiner.

* * *

Hands thrust deep in his pockets, shoulders hunched, and a scowl across his face, John walked out of the TravelTube at the Center, the place where most Hyperspace High pupils hung out in their free time.

A few feet away, his friends were leaning over one of the many balconies, watching students splashing in the waters of the small lake below. Tall trees with pink, yellow, and purple leaves towered over them, stretching toward the enormous clear dome above.

Dodging through the crowd, past Technomancer's Gamestation and nodding at a few of the beings who wished him good morning, John slouched up to Kaal and Emmie.

"Hi, John," Emmie started brightly. Seeing the look on his face, her own smile fell. "Oh no," she continued.

"Bad luck," said Kaal, clapping him on the shoulder with a strength that made John stagger. "Archivus Major's not going to be the same without you."

Unable to keep up the act, John grinned. "I made it!" he yelled. "I *passed*. I'm coming after all. I almost kissed the Examiner when it told me!"

Kaal's and Emmie's faces lit up.

"*Awesome!*" Kaal yelped with joy, his wings flapping as they always did when he was excited. "Hey, get off him, Tarz. Leave the Earthling alone."

Reluctantly, John disentangled himself from

Emmie's hug. "So," he said. "I believe there was talk of a celebration breakfast."

"Special treat," said Kaal. "The new Seefood restaurant on balcony eighteen. It's tough to get in, but I put our names on the list there two days ago."

"That sounds cool," John said. "I love seafood. Never had it for breakfast before, but, hey, I've never been examined by a freaky floating robot before, either."

"You're going to love it," said Kaal, clapping him on the shoulder again. "Especially after all that Earth muck you eat."

Balcony eighteen was on the highest level of the Center, reached by a revolving, clear TravelTube. It was the first time John had been up so high and he looked at the view with awe, wondering what his friends from Earth would say if they were here.

Like a vast shopping mall, the Center was ringed with balconies, each with its own brightly lit shops and cafés. Even at this time of the morning, it was bustling with beings from every corner of the galaxy. Students who looked as though they had been constructed almost entirely from electronic parts were deep in conversation with creatures that flitted about on dragonfly wings. Some students hovered in anti-gravity suits, others had specially made helmets that allowed them to breathe the atmosphere of their home planets. The strangest being reminded John of a swarm of bees.

"Here we are: Seefood," said Kaal, as the TravelTube door slid open.

John stared. Across the passageway was a restaurant. Above its door, outlined in pink neon lights, a huge eye winked at him. "Um . . . what's this?" he asked nervously.

"Seefood," said Emmie, making for the door. "You know: eyeballs. They've got Murlian Snowbeast eyeballs, eyeballs of the Deplar Flat Tiger, Pord eyeballs — every kind of eyeball you can think of."

"She's joking, isn't she?" John asked hopefully, looking up at Kaal.

"Why would you think that?" replied Kaal, confused. "I'm having eyeballs of the Twilight Blink Lizard. Absolutely delicious."

Stomach already heaving, John followed his friends into the restaurant.

"Table for three, Zepp," said Kaal.

"Certainly, Kaal," Zepp's voice replied. "The table at the back of the restaurant has been reserved for you."

The three friends slipped into MorphSeat stools. "And what will you be having this fine morning?" asked Zepp. "May I recommend the Zabda eyes, smothered with retina-fire hot sauce."

Feeling queasier by the minute, John leaned on the circular silver table and tried to take his mind off eyeballs by looking around. It didn't help. There were pictures of eyeballs everywhere, as well as decorative jars full of eyeballs and a huge glass eyeball slowly spinning in the middle of the restaurant. Not for the first time, he cursed himself for forgetting about his alien friends' disgusting eating habits.

"Hmm. The Zabda eyes sound good. But do you have Derrilian Twilight Blink Lizard?" asked Kaal.

"Of course. Seefood has eyeballs from every planet you could name," Zepp replied. "And for you, Emmie?"

"The Zabda eyes sound good. I'll start with those," said Emmie.

"*Excellent* choice. How about you, John?" Zepp asked.

"We don't eat eyeballs on Earth," said John faintly.

"Actually, that's not true," replied the computer. "Many Earthlings enjoy sheep's eyes. Would you like to try some?" Zepp stopped. "Oh, I just checked. We don't have any sheep's eyes. You could try the Jink-Jink eyeballs; they taste almost the same."

"Is there any chance you could just make me an omelet?"

"*An omelet?*"

"You know: eggs, a splash of milk, some salt and pepper, butter . . . "

"I know what an omelet is, John, but are you sure you don't want to be a little more adventurous?"

"What are *erggs?*" Emmie interrupted.

"Eggs," Zepp answered. "They come from birds' bottoms."

Emmie and Kaal glanced at each other in shock.

"How utterly revolting," Emmie whispered, managing to sound as sick as John felt. "You Earthlings don't *eat* them, do you?"

"Yes," said John firmly. "We do. I'll have an omelet, *please*, Zepp."

"If you're sure. I could put some eyeballs on the side if you like."

A few moments later, compartments opened in the smooth surface of the table. Dishes containing the food rose from beneath.

John inspected his plate to make sure that no eyeballs had been hidden beneath his omelet, then hunched over and kept his own eyes on his breakfast.

Even so, he couldn't help catching a glimpse

of large sundae glasses piled high with eyeballs and drenched in blood-red sauce. Making noises of hungry delight, Kaal and Emmie dug into their food.

Silently, John thanked his stars that they were both too busy eating to notice where he was looking. Listening to the wet, slightly crunchy, slurping noises from across the table, he soon began to wish he could stuff his fingers in his ears.

"What's wrong with John?" asked Gobi-san-Art, who was sitting with Lishtig at the next table. "Why's he sitting like that?"

"You okay, John?" Kaal's voice sounded as if he was speaking with his mouth full.

Shielding his eyes from the view with one hand, John lifted his head. "Fine," he said. "Slight headache. Must be the stress of the examination this morning."

"Try a Zabda eyeball," said Emmie, holding one under his nose on the end of a prong.

"Thanks, but no thanks," John choked, waving it away quickly. "I'm full."

"Anyway," Gobi-san-Art cut in, his gravelly voice unmistakable. "What do you want to see first on Archivus Major? I'm hoping it's the Grand Diamond of Iona. Apparently, it's as big as a K'laar Whale, glitters like a Dazzle Star, and is carved with pipes that make music when there's a breeze."

"*Boring*," interrupted Lishtig. "If we get the chance, I'm going straight to the Hall of Games. They have a full-scale Darl Labyrinth complete with deathtraps. I bet the Omega-bots won't let us play, though," he finished, sounding disappointed. "What about you, Riley?"

"After the last field trip, I just want to keep out of trouble," replied John, staring at a few inches of tabletop. "Nice, safe, *boring* exhibits suit me fine. No volcanoes."

Kaal chuckled. "I can't wait to get to the Star Dragon," he said. "Emmie, you have to get a 4-D photo of me standing next to it. My dad is going to be so jealous."

"I want to go straight to the Goran-Subo battleground," said Emmie firmly.

"No way. There's tons of way more interesting things to see. Mmmm, these eyeballs are *really* good."

Stomach churning, John heard a squelch as the Derrilian popped another into his mouth.

"Are you sure you're all right, John?" asked Kaal. "You look like you're going to be sick."

"It's nothing," John croaked. "I'm all right, honestly."

A chime sounded.

"Would students going to Archivus Major

please make their way to exit port alpha immediately," announced Zepp's voice. "We will be launching in thirty minutes."

Never before had John been so grateful to leave a restaurant. Making a mental note never to let his friends take him out to eat again, he jumped to his feet. "We'd better go," he said. "No time to waste."

"I haven't finished my eyeballs," said Kaal. "Maybe I could wrap them in a napkin for later . . . John, hey, *John*. Wait for us!"

CHAPTER 6

The disgusting breakfast pushed to the back of his mind, John stood outside the changing rooms with his chattering classmates.

When he looked out of a window at the stars, John felt a familiar wave of excitement surge through him. His forehead creased as he tried to put his finger on exactly what the feeling was.

Then he smiled. It was just like going on a family vacation. His dad always made the family get up ridiculously early and pile into the car while it was still dark outside.

We're in space. It's always dark outside, he reminded himself.

John felt a sudden pang of homesickness. He missed his parents. Plus, he missed the feeling of the sun on his face. Even though he had made good friends at Hyperspace High, he missed the company of other humans. Half the time he couldn't understand what the aliens around him were talking about. Although the ship's systems modified sound waves to translate every word that anyone spoke into each being's native language, the other students talked constantly about technologies, planets, and beings that he had never heard of.

Suddenly, the changing-room door opened and John was brought back to the present.

"Pay attention," barked Sergeant Jegger,

entering with the headmaster and Ms. Vartexia at his side.

Instantly, the buzz of conversation died. No one ever disobeyed the sergeant.

"As you know, you will be spared my company on this trip," Jegger continued, "for which I am sure you are all truly grateful. But before you go, I want to remind you that you are flying extremely valuable Xi-Class Privateers. I want every single one of them back in one piece. Are you listening, Riley?"

"Sir, yes sir," John said quickly.

"Good. So no fancy maneuvers or risk-taking. Yes, I'm looking at you, Talliver. Now, you'll be piloting your own craft through deep space, which means you'll need to be suited up. When I call your name, go to a cubicle and change into the SecondSkin pilot's suit you find there, then report to me for flight checks. Lishtig ar Steero, first cubicle. Bareon, second cubicle, John Riley, third cubicle . . . "

Adrenaline pumping, John ran a hand down the silver and red spacesuit hanging in his cubicle. It felt like living rubber and rippled beneath his fingers. On a metal bench beside it sat a high-tech helmet, a pair of knee-high boots, and gauntlet gloves, all in the same colors. Quickly, he climbed out of his clothes and transferred them to a bag, then slipped into the spacesuit. It tightened, flowing around him, shaping itself to fit his body exactly.

It was the strangest sensation John had ever felt. Pulling on the boots and gloves, he looked in the mirror.

It was immediately clear why the material was called SecondSkin. There was barely a wrinkle in it as he moved. The suit fit him like it had been sprayed on. He pulled on the helmet, feeling the same sensation as the foam-like interior molded itself to his head.

"Optimum body temperature reached," said a quiet voice in the helmet. "Processing oxygen. Suit ready."

"John," he murmured to himself as he gazed at his reflection, "you are looking *awesome.*"

"Riley, what are you doing in there?" Jegger shouted from outside. "Knitting your own spacesuit? Get to the hangar deck on the double."

On deck, Jegger marched up and down the line of pilots, checking that each of their suits was fitted correctly.

He paid special attention to Ms. Vartexia's suit. John wondered briefly if all of the staff members knew she had a tendency to make mistakes.

Lifting the visor of his helmet, John turned

to Kaal to make a comment. His friend was looking somewhere else: at the headmaster.

"Something interesting?" John asked.

"It's nothing," Kaal said. "Well, it's just a little weird, that's all."

"What's weird?"

Kaal looked down at him. "The headmaster *never* leaves the ship. Even for vacations."

John shrugged. "Maybe he feels like a break. He seemed pretty excited about visiting Archivus Major."

"Maybe you're right, but it is strange," Kaal said. "Makes you wonder if he knows something is going to happen."

Everyone on Hyperspace High knew that the headmaster could see into the future.

As he had explained to John a few weeks earlier, his visions weren't always clear and sometimes only showed him events that *might* happen, but suddenly John understood Kaal's concern.

"You think something bad is going to happen?" he asked, starting to feel worried. The last time he had left Hyperspace High, the class had nearly been killed on Zirion Beta.

"Kaal's just being a worry-Wigartian," Emmie cut in. "We're going to the most heavily guarded, secure planet in the galaxy. What could possibly go wrong?"

Satisfied that all the SecondSkin spacesuits were functioning correctly, Sergeant Jegger paced to the front of the row. "You will board your craft and launch one at a time," he ordered. "Join your classmates flying in formation alongside Hyperspace High before setting on a course for Archivus Major. Get to it."

With these last orders, Jegger marched smartly off the deck. Within moments, the hangar would be emptied of air and the bay doors opened. Beyond was space.

Gulp.

With his heart in his mouth, John climbed into the pilot seat of his Privateer and readied himself for takeoff.

Don't mess this up, Riley, he told himself silently. *Whatever you do, do NOT mess this up.*

"Computer, disengage docking locks, start engines, and display speed," he said, ignoring a fresh wave of anxiety.

"Affirmative. Ready to launch, John Riley," replied the computer. The Privateer hummed with energy.

From the corner of his eye, John saw a movement. He glanced around to see Kaal holding out three fingers — the Derrilian thumbs up, John had learned. In reply, John mimed wiping sweat from his forehead.

Ahead of them, the bay doors slid open noiselessly.

Jegger's voice filled the craft: "Ms. Vartexia, would you lead? The headmaster will bring up the rear."

"Certainly, Sergeant."

John watched in disbelief as the Elvian teacher's craft swooped smoothly out into space. Ms. Vartexia, it seemed, had hidden talents.

One by one the ships took off, some wobbling a little, but all successfully joining Ms. Vartexia's ship. When John's turn came, he tried to remember how he had felt during the examination.

"You are a part of the machine," he muttered to himself, touching the controls. The Privateer lifted from the deck.

He moved his fingers. "Computer, match velocity of Hyperspace High plus fifty," he said, as the ship zoomed right through the open bay door.

"Velocity plus fifty."

Gently, John turned the craft so that it was heading along the same course as Hyperspace High and fell in with the small line of waiting ships.

"Launch successful," said the computer.

John looked around. Taking up most of the view was the vast, elegant bulk of Hyperspace High, glittering with thousands of viewing windows. *We're like mosquitoes flying alongside an eagle*, he thought.

The headmaster's voice broke in on his thoughts. "Thank you, Sergeant. I'll take them from here."

"Jegger signing off. Safe trip."

"Initiate LightFast engines and set course for Archivus Major," the headmaster told the fleet.

"Computer: display astrometric location, initiate hyperspace engines, and set course for Archivus Major," John ordered.

Complicated readings appeared on the ship's shell to the right of John's view, along with a detailed diagram of Archivus Major.

"Coordinates laid in, ready to jump," the computer told him.

"On my mark," said Lorem. "In three, two, one . . . *go*."

"Initiate jump." John was hardly able to breathe, he was so excited.

Instantly, the small spaceship leaped forward. From the sci-fi movies he'd seen, John expected that a leap to faster-than-light speed would mean all the stars streaming toward him at once, while G-force pressed him back in his seat. In reality, there was a lurching feeling of suddenly reaching a great speed. Hyperspace

High disappeared in a blink. Then everything was almost disappointingly normal. Stars passed by — that much was true — but there were no special effects. John had asked Kaal about it once and had been answered with a bewildering speech about dampening fields, quantum astrophysics, and differential drives. John hadn't understood a word of it.

"All present and correct, Ms. Vartexia," the headmaster's voice said. "Arrival at Archivus Major in three hours and eight minutes. Students, you may now activate communication relays and talk among yourselves."

Kaal's voice came through the ship's intercom immediately. "You get a great view from the cockpit of a Privateer, don't you?" he said.

John had to agree. In most of the ships he'd flown in, he'd only been able to look through windows. But since the Xi-Class Privateer's whole shell was transparent, it felt like he was floating through space.

John felt himself relaxing as he looked around with new wonder. Not for the first time, he had to remind himself that this was no dream. He really was piloting a spaceship through the galaxy hundreds of light-years from his own world.

"You can magnify stuff, too," Emmie chipped in, as they passed through a solar system. "Take a closer look at the planet to the left."

"Computer: magnify view of the planet at coordinates seventeen point six point zero zero two. . . . *Wow.*"

John gazed in wonder as a view of the planet's surface appeared on the ship's skin. A vast ocean of skyscraper-tall waves was being lashed by a hurricane. Here and there, huge spouts of water whirled into the planet's upper atmosphere.

"Hey, magnify twenty-three point nine point three zero four," Kaal interrupted.

John gave the command. A new view filled his screen: a spaceship shaped like an enormous disc and blazing with light. Through a clear dome, similar to Hyperspace High's, John glimpsed blue water lined with sandy beaches and lush greenery.

"Yarvene pleasure cruiser," Kaal told him. "Very, very expensive way to get around the galaxy."

Lishtig's voice broke into the conversation. "Guys, have you seen the *huuuuge* mining ship? Mordant says it's one of his dad's mallux prospectors. No wonder his family's so rich."

Within minutes, every spaceship was connected. With the exception of Mordant, who was still sulking about missing the Vaporball Championship, the Hyperspace High students chatted happily to one another as the fleet of Privateers powered through space.

Now and then, the headmaster and Ms. Vartexia chipped in with interesting facts and information about planets they were passing. Every half hour, John's computer gave a status update. The ships were crossing light-years in less time than it took to drive across his hometown during rush hour.

"Now approaching Archivus Major," the computer reported eventually. "Dropping out of hyperspace. Landing procedures initiated. Prepare for return to manual."

"Affirmative. Return to manual." Ahead was the planet that John had last seen on the 3-D screens in Ms. Vartexia's classroom. In orbit around it was a network of security satellites, each — John knew — heavily armed to prevent unauthorized landings on the planet.

"Formation alpha twelve," Lorem's voice commanded briskly. "Take positions. We'll be landing one at a time. Each craft will be escorted in by Omega-bots. Do not be alarmed when you see them. Take it slow and remember what Sergeant Jegger taught you."

Gritting his teeth, John took the controls again, his anxiety returning.

Takeoff was always nerve-wracking, but landing was harder, and this time he wasn't making a simple approach to the hangar deck of Hyperspace High.

This time he would be entering the atmosphere of a strange planet and landing at an unfamiliar docking port.

In an instant, the Privateer's cockpit was filled with bright yellow light, flashing from the nearest satellite. John covered his eyes in confusion.

"The DNA scan," the headmaster said reassuringly. "It will be over soon."

As Lorem had predicted, the light blinked off two seconds later. John watched as Ms. Vartexia's ship peeled and dived toward the planet below. His palms felt sweaty in the SecondSkin gloves. As the planet revolved beneath him, John caught himself wondering what he would be doing if he had returned to Earth and gone to Wortham Court.

Nothing as exciting as this.

Lorem's voice announced, "John Riley, you're clear to land."

"Computer, display docking guides." Data appeared on the screen, and the landing beacon flashed in the center. "Here we go," John muttered, as his fingers moved across the touchpads. The Privateer turned slightly, lining up with the docking sight. John dropped the craft's nose and dived toward the planet.

The small spaceship shook as it hit the atmosphere. Clouds streamed by, cutting visibility to zero. With only the indicators on the ship's shell to guide him, John felt panic rising.

Too fast, too fast!

He was through the clouds. Beneath, land was rushing up to meet him: a patchwork of different environments and sprawling building complexes. Outside, something moved to take position by the window.

John turned his head and looked straight into the barrel of a gun.

CHAPTER 7

Near the ship, a bulky machine — at least ten feet tall — was keeping perfect pace with John's Privateer. Its eight arms each held a heavy warp gun. From what little he had learned of galactic weapons, John knew that just one warp gun was more than capable of reducing the Privateer to atomic particles.

Currently, *two* warp guns were pointing directly at him.

His jaw dropped open inside the helmet.

He tried to shout, but nothing came out of his mouth.

Somewhere in the back of his mind, a small voice told him to stop staring at the machine and to concentrate on landing.

With effort, he returned his attention toward the ground. The dock was just ahead. He could see students milling around their landed ships already. John suddenly realized that in the shock of seeing the Omega-bot, he'd forgotten to cut the speed.

I'm coming in too fast! he screamed in his head. *I'm going to crash. I'm going to CRASH!*

Terrified, John squeezed his eyes shut. Zepp's words echoed in John's head. "Believe in yourself."

He opened his eyes.

No. I'm not going to crash. Not today.

Seconds away from smashing into the

landing pad, a look of grim determination crossed John's face. Moving over the touchpad skillfully, his right hand brought the front of the Privateer up. His left reduced the speed quickly but smoothly.

Still too fast. Too late now . . .

Numbers flickered on the shell screen by his head: twenty-five feet from the ground, fifteen, ten, five.

The Privateer landed with the lightest of bumps.

"Awesome landing, John. Really, I don't know why you were so worried about the examination."

John blinked as Emmie's voice came through the craft's intercom. He stared wildly about him, hardly daring to believe that he had landed safely. Yet the ship was resting on the landing strip, neatly at the end of a row.

Somehow, he had managed to land without killing himself, or anyone else.

Believe in yourself.

"Maybe," he whispered. "Or maybe it was luck. Don't start getting cocky just yet, Riley."

Beside him, another Privateer landed, bouncing and skidding to a halt a good distance from where it was supposed to be. Seconds later, Kaal clambered out, shaking his head.

Leaning back in his seat, John felt a grin of relief spread across his face. He was alive. And even if it had been luck rather than skill, he had still made a landing good enough to impress Emmie. "Computer," he said. "Engage docking protocols, shut down engines, and let me out of here."

"Affirmative, John Riley."

Jumping out of the craft, John pulled off his helmet, running a hand through his mop of blond hair as he walked over to the gaggle of students thronging around Ms. Vartexia. Behind, four Omega-bots stood guard, watching every movement through glowing green electronic eyes, warp guns held ready. Telling himself the machines were there to guard the exhibits, not to execute visitors, John tried to ignore them.

The Elvian teacher was trying to keep order, but no one was listening. Around her, backs were slapped; hands, tentacles, and claws smacked together in high-fives.

Mordant, John noticed, was standing on the edge of the group with only G-Vez buzzing around his shoulders.

"A superb landing, young master," the droid droned, sounding quite unimpressed. Since no one else was congratulating Mordant, it extended a small arm for a brief high-five.

"Very cool moves, John!" Emmie yelled as

John approached. "Too bad Jegger didn't see you: he'd be proud."

"Don't you dare tell him about my landing," said Kaal, jogging across the landing pad to join them. "He'll never let me pilot a spaceship again."

"It wasn't that bad," Emmie said, laughing. "Bareon's was worse. Wasn't it, Bareon?"

"I hardly touched Queelin's ship," Bareon snapped.

"It didn't feel like that from the inside!" Queelin shouted back, her antennae twitching furiously. "I was thrown halfway across the dock."

"You were lucky the whole dock isn't a smoking crater in the ground," said John seriously. "I totally freaked out when I saw the Omega-bot flying next to me. Thought I was going to crash."

"Here we all are, safe and sound," the headmaster cut in brightly as he climbed out of his own Privateer. "And my goodness, such a beautiful day, too."

John realized that he was squinting and that his skin felt pleasantly warm. For the first time since he had left Earth, he could feel a sun's rays on his face, the warmth of a star halfway across the galaxy from his own.

Looking up, he saw white clouds drifting across a blue sky. In the distance, snowy mountain peaks glittered in the sunlight. Further down, waterfalls of melting snow poured through a thick jungle. Not far from the docking port was a wide lake.

John's grin returned, along with the vacation feeling he'd had in the changing room at Hyperspace High. Archivus Major was a beautiful planet.

"Since we only have two days and a whole world of wonders to see, I suggest we get started immediately," Lorem continued, rubbing his hands together in glee. "We'll walk to the Mars Dust Storm exhibit. This should be of special interest to you, John. Mars, as you know, is your own planet's closest neighbor."

* * *

"Mars!" Ms. Vartexia called out. "One of the galaxy's most interesting worlds. Despite the planet's hostile environment, its people achieved hyperspace technology very quickly and led the way in forming the first Galactic Council."

The group walked across a bridge that looked like it was made from glass, followed by the ever-present Omega-bots.

Already, John was finding it easier to ignore

the menacing, silent machines. They were quickly becoming part of the scenery.

Ahead stood a massive, box-like gray building.

"Obviously, none of us are Martians, so we will have to wear protective suits," Ms. Vartexia continued, with a sharp look at John.

He smiled, remembering that the only reason he was at Hyperspace High was because she had mistaken him for a Martian prince.

"What is this place?" he asked Kaal a few minutes later, while they both pulled white all-in-one suits with face masks over their SecondSkins.

Every student had been issued a ThinScreen guide at the dock, and Kaal was currently flicking through his.

"It says here that Mars Dust Storm exactly simulates the conditions on Mars forty million years ago," the Derrilian replied. "I guess it's supposed to give visitors an idea of how hard it must have been for the Martians to build a civilization."

"Forty *million* years ago? Human beings on Earth only evolved about a quarter of a million years ago," John said.

Kaal looked down at him. "That explains a *lot*," he said, grinning.

John punched his friend on the shoulder. "At least we can land spaceships the right way," he shot back.

A few minutes later, the two of them lined up with the class in the main hall of Mars Dust Storm. In front of them was a vast desert of red sand and craggy rocks. Dotted here and there were pyramids that Ms. Vartexia told them had been towns and cities in the days before the Martian people had created new homes deep beneath the ground. Above, a vast ceiling screen showed a 3-D scene of dark skies and swirling clouds. The sun — *My sun*, John thought — looked small and weak.

"There's Earth," said Lorem quietly.

Following the headmaster's pointing finger, John saw what looked like a small star, blue against the dark background of space. Not twinkling, but shining with the constant light that meant it was a planet and not a distant sun.

Seeing his own planet gave John another pang of homesickness.

It's a hologram, not the real Earth, he told himself sternly.

"In a moment, the environment generators will start," said Ms. Vartexia. "When they do, we will make our way across the hall, stopping midway at the Pyramid of Tal-So-Ga."

A roaring sound began. Seconds later, John

was almost knocked off his feet by a gale that howled across the replica Mars.

Carried by the wind, red sand hissed against his face mask until he could see only a vague white shape that had been Kaal a few seconds before.

The temperature dropped quickly.

"Let's go!" shouted Ms. Vartexia over the storm. "Keep the person in front of you in sight at all times."

"You okay?" Kaal yelled over his shoulder, as they began the trek across the fake Martian landscape.

"No. Something really weird is happening!" John shouted back.

"What's the matter?"

"I'm actually *enjoying* a Hyperspace History class."

It was, John had to admit, a fascinating

experience. Every so often the wind dropped, giving just enough time to see rocky hills and pyramids in the distance. Then, all too quickly, it would resume a shrieking, sand-blasting howl that made conversation impossible.

Taking one tiring step after another against the gale, John tried to imagine what it must have been like to live on a planet like this.

No wonder they developed space travel quickly, he couldn't help thinking. *Probably couldn't leave fast enough.*

Inside the pyramid, a surprise was waiting for him. The furniture and decorations were almost exactly the same as he had seen in books about ancient Egypt. "Ms. Vartexia," he said excitedly, as the Elvian led the class inside. "Did the Martians ever contact human beings on Earth?"

"The Martians have been visiting your

planet for millions of years," the tall, blue-skinned teacher answered.

"But I thought they kept it a secret," John said. "Everything in this pyramid looks Egyptian."

Ms. Vartexia sighed. "That would have been the Martian king, Ram-Es-Izz the Bizarre. He had the strange idea that humans could be civilized and started trying to teach them. Of course, we now know that human beings are much too primit—"

"Many people still think that Ram-Es-Izz was a great king who saw potential in the people of Earth," Lorem interrupted. "I, for one, agree with him. Humans might be capable of great things."

"Ahh, yes. Yes indeed, Headmaster," said Ms. Vartexia quickly, looking from Lorem to John. "I'm sorry, I didn't mean to suggest that our John Riley is in any way primitive. I meant that —"

"Perhaps we should move on to the Pool of Ritual on the lower floor," said Lorem, cutting her off with a kind smile.

When the pyramid tour was over, the class headed back out into the dust storm. John took one last look behind him as he trudged across red rocks, watching as the great building disappeared in a cloud of sand.

For a moment, he wondered what would happen if he told his fellow humans about what he had learned there.

They'd lock me up and throw away the key.

By the time the class reached the exit, he was a little sad to be leaving the dust storm. Although it was fake, when the wind dropped he had been able to look up into the sky and see Earth shining down at him.

It had felt almost like being home.

"Well, Mars is as dull as a weekend on Darum Four," said Emmie Tarz, as the class piled out of the exit. "Whatever's next, I hope we can actually see where we're going."

"Yep. Seen one desolate, sandy planet, seen them all," Kaal agreed.

John grinned. It was difficult to be sad when Kaal and Emmie were around.

"Hey, you two, come on. That's my closest neighbor you're talking about. Wait . . . what is *that*?"

An alarm blared. Instantly, a door at the end of the corridor slammed shut. Students looked at each other, eyes wide, antennae twitching, and claws clicking nervously.

"What's going on?" demanded Lishtig.

"Quiet there," Ms. Vartexia ordered. "Thirteen, fourteen, fifteen . . . no. Headmaster, there are only fifteen students here. One is missing."

"Check again." Lorem's calm voice held a note of steel.

"Fifteen. I checked twice."

John looked around. "It's Mordant," he said quickly. "He's not here."

For a brief moment there was silence, then, in the distance, a voice: "Leave the young master alone. You don't know who you are dealing with. Master Talliver is a very important young man."

All eyes snapped to the Mars Dust Storm exit, where two Omega-bots emerged, holding Mordant between them. The warp guns had disappeared, as each of the machines' hands held a part of the black-haired boy. Mordant's face twisted in frustration as he tried to break free.

"Mordant Talliver," said Lorem icily. "Please tell me, immediately, what is going on here."

Instead of Mordant, it was G-Vez that answered. "If I may explain," said the little droid. "The young master took just a moment to observe —"

"I said *Mordant Talliver*," the headmaster roared. Gone was the kindly, cheerful old man. This was the voice of a powerful being whose word was law.

G-Vez fell silent. Mordant glared at the headmaster, then dropped his eyes.

An Omega-bot held out a portable HoloScreen in a metal claw. "Rule thirty-five A," it droned. "Communication technology is forbidden."

Lorem took the HoloScreen. "Ah, the Vaporball Championship," he said, looking down at it with disgust. "I should have known, but I didn't think that you would be quite so idiotic —"

"I was just trying to get the scores," Mordant interrupted sulkily.

"Be *quiet*," the headmaster commanded. "It is so foolish to break the rules here, of all places. Do you have any idea how much trouble you are in?"

Still glaring at the ground, Mordant shook his head. "You are lucky I don't expel you on the spot," Lorem bellowed. "All communication with other planets is banned on Archivus Major. You were told that a dozen times. It might interfere with the exhibits' delicate technology and cause a disaster."

Mordant said nothing.

"The Omega-bots will escort you back to your Privateer. I will decide what to do with you when we are back on Hyperspace High. In the meantime, you will stay in your ship until we leave this planet," Lorem finished.

"Can I at least have my HoloSc—"

"*Dismissed!*"

* * *

"I guess Mordant won't be seeing much of Archivus Major after all," said John, as the class and their two teachers settled on a shady hilltop outside the Mars Dust Storm building.

Looking into his bag, John pulled out a sandwich and peered at it. "BLT," he said, whistling. "With plenty of mayonnaise. My favorite. Thanks, Zepp."

"At least he'll have G-Vez to talk to," Emmie said with a giggle. "Two days will fly by."

"How come they let him bring the robo-servant anyway? I thought non-vital technology was banned," John said, biting off a huge chunk. "Mmmm, and *tons* of bacon," he mumbled.

"Non-invasive intrapersonal service technology, certified safe in any environment," Kaal answered, looking through his own bag. "Oh wow, Flarzworms. Nice one." He looked up to see John looking at him questioningly. "G-Vez has a containment field," he explained. "Nothing escapes it. The Omega-bots, too, I'd guess. It makes them as likely to interfere in other technologies as this Flarzworm," he finished, holding up the wriggling orange worm.

Face screwed up in revulsion, John turned his head away, only to find a sight just as unexpected. Over the Mars Dust Storm building, a Xi-Class Privateer was rising into the air.

The sandwich dropped from his hand. "Hey!" John shouted, getting to his feet and pointing. "Is that who I think it is?"

CHAPTER 8

As John watched the Privateer leave Archivus Major, he heard Lorem shout, "Mordant!"

Shielding his purple eyes from the sun, the headmaster glared at the rapidly disappearing spaceship with a face like thunder.

"I will expel him for this," he said, through clenched teeth.

"No. It can't be," said Ms. Vartexia, getting to her feet. "Surely, Headmaster, even Mordant Talliver wouldn't —"

"It cannot be anyone else," said Lorem grimly. "We are the only visitors on Archivus Major at present."

By now, the Privateer was a small dot in the sky. The class watched together in silent shock as the Privateer disappeared into the upper atmosphere.

"Why aren't the Omego-bots doing something to stop him?" asked John.

The headmaster glanced at him. "Their job is to protect the exhibits," he said. "Archivus Major's security systems are designed to stop people from getting in, not from leaving."

"Did you not see the possibility of this happening, Headmaster?" Ms. Vartexia asked, sounding confused.

"My visions of the future are not always clear," he replied, suddenly looking weary. "I sensed that a dangerous situation might develop on Archivus Major — that's why I came — but I must have been mistaken about the threat. I did not suspect for a second that Mordant Talliver would be the cause."

"What are we going to do now?" Ms. Vartexia asked. The Elvian teacher was still staring up at the sky. She began wringing her hands with worry.

With a deep sigh, Lorem turned to her. "This is very troublesome," he said. "But we have no choice. I *must* go after Mordant. Now he has gone, fragments of at least one possible future have fallen into place. I can see quite clearly that if I do not go after him, he will be in life-threatening danger."

"How will you know where to find him? He could be headed anywhere."

"I don't need to look into the future to know he will go straight to planet Plarz, where the

Vaporball Championship is being held," the headmaster replied.

"But what will *we* do?" Ms. Vartexia asked nervously.

The headmaster responded with a stern look. "Why, carry on with the visit, of course, Ms. Vartexia. The students are in your care. Now, if you will excuse me, the faster I follow, the faster I will find our stray."

"Yes, but . . . oh, I just don't know . . . but, but . . . "

"You will be fine!" Lorem shouted over his shoulder, as he strode away toward the dock. "Just follow the visitor guidelines and stay together. Remember: it is better to be safe than sorry."

As the headmaster's Privateer rose into the sky, the students looked at each other. Everyone was shocked.

"I can't believe Mordant just did that," said John.

Lishtig shook his head. "He's been acting weird since yesterday," he said. "The Vaporball Championship is all he's talked about. It's like he's totally obsessed."

"Hijacking a ship during a school trip is crazy, even for *him*," Bareon said, his enormous, black eyes blinking. "I mean, he's always breaking rules but he's really sneaky about it usually. He almost never actually gets *caught* doing anything wrong."

"Look, we all know that Mordant Talliver can be an idiot," said Emmie. "If he wants to get himself expelled, I'm not going to lose any sleep over it. The important thing is that he doesn't ruin the trip for the rest of us."

"That's true," said Kaal, peering at his ThinScreen. "Forget Mordant. It says here that we're not far from the Weapons Desert and there's a Shuttletube that will take us straight there. Sounds good to me."

"How about visiting the Goran-Subo battleground," Emmie suggested.

Kaal frowned at her. "Why are you so excited to go see the Goran-Subo battleground, Emmie?" he asked. "It's not like you to be interested in war."

Emmie shrugged, looking confused for a moment. "I . . . um . . . just want to take the photos. Get some extra credit. Besides, it is supposed to be spectacular."

At that moment, Queelin Temerate snatched the ThinScreen from Kaal's hands and looked through the pages.

"Wow, there are wild Feershcats and Flurbs in the jungle over there," she said, looking up with shining eyes. "Let's go on safari."

"Isn't there a spaceship exhibit?" John chipped in. "I'd love to see that."

Ms. Vartexia clapped. "Attention please, class," she said, sounding nervous.

The students turned to face her.

"Can we go to the spaceship exhibit, please?" John asked quickly.

"No, the jungle," someone else said.

"I want to see the Floating Pleasure Gardens of Vox Charm," said another student.

"The Star Dragon skeleton," put in another person.

"We've *got* to go to the Goran-Subo battlefield," Emmie said urgently.

"We could split up," Kaal suggested. "That way everyone would get to see what they wanted to see."

"Absolutely not," said the teacher firmly. "The headmaster instructed us to stay together, and that is exactly what we shall do. That means none of you is leaving my sight."

"But, Ms. Vartexia, why do we have to suffer because Mordant's being a total idiot?"

Ms. Vartexia chose not to hear Queelin Temerate's question. Opening her own guidebook, she said, "Ahh, here's just the thing: the Rock Gallery."

"Rock music?" asked John hopefully.

"Rocks and minerals from every corner of the galaxy," answered the teacher. "It will be excellent for your understanding of galactic geology. Doctor Graal *will* be pleased."

Her announcement was met by a chorus of groans. "Who cares what Doctor Slobber thinks," muttered Lishtig.

Only Gobi-san-Art was happy. "I *love* rocks," he said, a grin stretching across his face. "Rocks are awesome."

"That's settled, then," said Ms. Vartexia, closing the book with a snap. "Follow me to the Shuttletube. Keep together and do not touch *anything*."

* * *

"Wow: a rock," said Emmie, standing on a gravel path with her hands on her hips. "It's just so . . . so *exactly* the same as the last rock we looked at."

"Not really," said Gobi in a very serious tone. "The last rock we looked at was a perfect example of sedimentary histracite. This specimen is taurite, but it contains a vein of mallux."

Emmie rolled her eyes.

"Rock," she said, pointing at it. Turning, she pointed at the rock next to it. "Rock," she repeated. She shook her head and added, "And that, Gobi, is all I know, or ever want to know, about rocks."

"You're missing out on some really, really interesting —"

"Please stop," Emmie grumbled. "I am *so* bored of this. A whole planet stacked with the most amazing stuff in the universe, and we're staring at some lumps of old rock. What's wrong with Ms. Vartexia?"

"Maybe we should give her a break," suggested John. "It can't be easy for her, being in charge on her own, and you know what she's like."

Kaal nodded. "You mean like bringing Earthlings back to Hyperspace High instead of Martian princes?" he asked. "That sort of thing?"

"*Exactly.* Accident prone. She's probably

scared that something awful will happen and she'll lose her job."

"Hey, you guys," Lishtig interrupted, running across the gravel and whooping. "I've just had a word with Ms. Vartexia. She's got a whole heap of fun lined up for later."

"*Really?*" said Emmie, eagerly. "Are we going to the battlefield next?"

"No, but . . . wait for it . . . we're going to the Rare Moss Garden."

Closing her eyes, Emmie groaned again. "I am going to kill Mordant Talliver," she whispered.

As the afternoon passed, the class visited one dull exhibit after another.

The only interesting part is the Shuttletube ride in between, John thought, leaning back in his seat. Something like an ultra-modern train, the Shuttletube rocketed at high speed through the clear tubes that snaked across the landscape of Archivus Major.

It was an exhilarating ride. The only downside was that the Shuttletube gave the students a clear view of everything they were missing.

John had been especially disappointed when the Shuttletube swept past a vast hangar that seemed to cover hundreds of square miles. Kaal had leaned over and told him it was the spaceship exhibit.

John was feeling restless and grouchy. He wasn't alone. In the Rare Moss Garden, the only excitement had been an Omega-bot's alarm siren going off in Kaal's ear.

The Derrilian had been about to touch a thousand-year-old Pestra Moss while the huge robot guard was right behind him. Its alarm had been so loud that green ooze had leaked from Kaal's ear, which had meant another uninteresting visit, this time to the medical center.

The Rare Moss Garden seemed like a rollercoaster of thrills compared to the Chong Gallery, though. The ancient Vyranian artist Javvid Chong had spent his entire career painting pictures of the same small brown moon.

At first, John thought the hundreds of paintings, each only slightly different from the next, must be some kind of joke. Ms. Vartexia, however, had patiently explained that Chong's paintings made important statements about art and reality.

By the time he had looked at the thirtieth moon painting, John had become certain he was losing his own grip on reality and wondered if this was what the teacher had meant. Fortunately, even Ms. Vartexia was quickly bored by the gallery and hustled the class along to the next dreary exhibit.

By the time the sun began to set, John had stopped even looking up when someone pointed out yet another wonder the Shuttletube was passing by.

The whole class had long since discovered that there was no point in asking Ms. Vartexia to stop; she was obstinately refusing to take them anywhere that might be even the slightest bit dangerous.

"Where next?" John asked. He sighed.

"Huh? Excuse me?" Kaal leaned in toward him, his ear stuffed with spacecloud wadding. "What did you say?"

"I said, *where next?*" John yelled. It occurred to him that now, talking to Kaal had suddenly become almost exactly like talking to his grandfather.

The Derrilian shrugged. "Gave up caring at the moss place," he answered.

"I'm hungry," said John.

"What?"

"I'M *HUNGRY*!"

Farther down the Shuttletube, Ms. Vartexia broke off a conversation she had been having with Werril, and looked over at them. "There's no need to shout, John Riley," she said primly. "As it happens," she continued, "we are now on our way to Optical Orbit, the restaurant where we will be eating tonight. I am told it is quite a treat."

"Thank goodness," said Emmie. "Food, then bed, and then only one more day of this nightmare to get through."

John grunted in agreement. Sitting back, he watched as the scenery turned to ice and snow and the sun slowly went down.

"This is more *like* it," he said ten minutes later. The Shuttletube had stopped at the front gates of a crystal sphere the size of a palace. It twinkled with the reflected light of Archivus Major's twin moons.

"Optical Orbit," announced the Shuttletube's automatic voice.

Ms. Vartexia led the way up a wide staircase to the perfectly circular door. "It's one of the most famous restaurants in the universe," she said.

Inside, John gazed around in wonder.

"Sheesh," whispered Emmie next to him. "My dad has taken me to some really fancy restaurants, but I've never seen anything like *this*."

At the far end of the entrance hall, a fire of pure blue flame roared in a magnificent fireplace.

On either side, sweeping staircases climbed to a gallery that circled the great room. A mind-twisting light show moved across the spherical walls, while glowing orbs rose and fell to the beat.

It's like being in a giant lava lamp, John thought.

CHAPTER 9

"This place is incredible," he said out loud, nudging Kaal.

"Huh? What?" his friend replied. "You think the plates are *inedible*?"

John was so busy staring around, he didn't notice the silver cart rolling across the floor until it stopped right in front of the group.

"Good evening, honored guests" the box-on-wheels said in a high-pitched voice. "You must be the party from Hyperspace High."

"Yes, that's right," Ms. Vartexia said, nodding. "I believe we have a table reserved already, but I'm afraid we are missing two from our group."

"That is quite all right," the cart replied. "You are the only visiting party on the planet at the moment and we have arranged everything for your most supreme enjoyment. Please, follow me."

Turning away, the cart-waiter trundled across the floor to a large, round table surrounded by MorphSeats and set for eighteen diners. In the center of the table was another crystal ball that looked like a smaller version of the restaurant itself. Blobs of brightly colored light moved through it.

Small name cards told each student where to sit. Silently, another cart on wheels rolled forward. A hatch opened in its side and long metal arms emerged, removing two of the place settings.

"They've really thought about this," John whispered to Emmie, as he looked around the table. In front of him was a place setting that included a knife, fork, and spoon. Emmie's place setting had the metal prong that Sillarans used for eating. Kaal's had the Derrilian tarb, which looked like a cross between a large spoon and a fork.

"Thank you for noticing," purred the waiter. Its own metal arm emerged and the machine clicked its fingers. Instantly, words appeared in the air above John's plate: the menu. "At Optical Orbit we pride ourselves on providing the perfect dining experience for every guest," the cart told him. "Everything must be exactly right."

Glancing at the menu, John almost jumped

with surprise. It listed all his favorite foods: spare ribs, cheeseburgers, sweet and sour chicken, lasagna, and more. In the side-order section he found fries, onion rings, coleslaw: again, everything he loved.

"How did you —" he began.

The cart made a noise that sounded to John like a little laugh. "We have our ways, sir," it said.

"Cool, they have Derrilian Colca," said Kaal, as the waiter rolled away. "And Nish Crab, and . . . hey, it's all my favorite things."

"Mine, too," said Emmie. "How do they do that?"

"Most likely they take information from Archivus Major's DNA scanners and cross-reference it to a database of your home planet's most popular meals," explained Lishtig. "Look, there is Trilbean Stew on my menu. I'm the only one on the entire planet of Slarce who *hates* Trilbean Stew."

"I'm terribly sorry, sir," said the cart-waiter, returning to the table. "There's been a mistake." It snapped its metal fingers again. The words over Lishtig's place setting changed. "That menu was for a Slarcian visitor we had last week. This one," he said, placing a new menu in front of Lishtig, "has Lormfry instead of Trilbean Stew."

"But . . . but Lormfry's my *absolute* favorite," spluttered Lishtig.

"We know, sir. We know. Now, may I take your orders?"

After changing his mind at least thirty times, John finally decided on spare ribs, followed by macaroni and cheese, with chocolate cake for dessert.

At the end of the meal, he leaned back in

his MorphSeat, patting his stomach. "That was the best food I've had since I left Earth," he said happily. "I mean, the cafeteria on Hyperspace High isn't bad, but that chocolate cake was the best ever."

"Thank you, sir," the cart-waiter replied, taking John's empty plate and adding it to a teetering pile on the top of its flat surface. "I shall pass your compliments on to the robo-chef."

"Have you seen Ms. Vartexia?" whispered Emmie. She nodded across the table, where the teacher was huddled over a large bowl of blue Elvian spaghetti. "That's her third bowl."

"For someone so thin, she really loves food," replied John. He watched in awe as Ms. Vartexia shoveled in another mouthful. "Look, she's calling the waiter over. She can't be asking for another bowl . . . whoa! She *is*."

Kaal leaned in, turning his good ear toward John to find out what he and Emmie were whispering about.

"I've never seen an Elvian eat like that," he told them. "Normally, an Elvian portion size wouldn't be big enough to feed a Derrilian Smallworm."

Eventually, however, Ms. Vartexia managed to fill herself.

"Now," squeaked the waiter as he took her empty bowl, "we have organized a special event for our guests from Hyperspace High: a private show by Great Red Spot."

"What on Earth is this?" asked John, baffled.

A small stage had been set up. Four gently glimmering balls of gas hovered there. Twanging, high-pitched noises filled the air. He couldn't tell how the strange sounds were being made.

"It's music," said Emmie.

"Are you sure?"

Emmie stared at him. "Of course I'm sure. Don't you have music on your planet?" Before John could answer, she continued, "Great Red Spot is an incredible group. I love this song. It's called 'Take Me to Your Leader.'"

"Shouldn't it have, you know, a tune?" John asked.

"A tune? How very primiti— old-fashioned," Emmie said, smiling. "Let me guess, on Earth the musicians play hollowed out logs with the bones of their enemies, right?"

"On Earth, the musicians play music you can actually dance to," John retorted. He looked at Kaal for support. Since they had started sharing a room, Kaal had heard a lot of the Earth music that John and Zepp both loved.

But this time, Kaal was no help at all. The

Derrilian was standing and holding out a hand to Emmie. "Come on, Tarz," he said. "Let's show the Earthling how to dance."

John almost choked with laughter as the two of them hit the flashing dance floor. Kaal, wings outstretched, looked like he was treading across hot coals. Every so often he would leap in the air, yowling.

Emmie, meanwhile, simply lifted one leg in the air and hopped up and down while flapping her hands.

Thinking they must be kidding around, John looked around the table, but no one else was laughing. In fact, more of the students were now getting up and joining Kaal and Emmie. As John spluttered in disbelief, Bareon bent over until he was clutching his own ankles and started shaking his backside in the air.

"Are you not dancing, John Riley?"

Biting back fresh gales of laughter, John looked across the table to see Ms. Vartexia looking at him. Covering her mouth, she burped. "Excuse me. As I was about to say: we Elvians do not dance — we don't have the knees for it — but I believe it is a pleasurable experience. Why don't you join your classmates?"

John opened his mouth to tell her that his classmates looked ridiculous and the music was dreadful. Then he stopped himself. *Why not*, he thought. *If you can't beat them, join them*.

"Show us some Earth dancing!" Emmie shouted over the music as John arrived on the dance floor.

Trying not to giggle, he struck a pose he'd once seen in an old movie called *Saturday Night Fever*. Spinning on the spot, he found a beat somewhere in the bizarre music and began doing another funny move. Arms folded, he squatted close to the floor, kicking his legs out as quickly as he could.

"Wow!" shouted Emmie. "Great moves. You Earthlings can *really* dance."

"You haven't seen anything yet," John replied. Raising his arms, he tried a new move over the polished floor.

Lishtig stared at him, jaw hanging open. "B-but it looks like you're walking forward, when you're actually going b-backward," he said with a gasp.

"Yeah, on Earth we call it the Moonwalk," said John, grinning.

"But that's just silly!" yelled Kaal over the music. "Moons generally have a lower gravitational force than most planets, so a 'moonwalk' would look more like this . . ." He leaped into the air, making large, slow movements.

John rolled his eyes. "It's just a name, Kaal!" he called back. "Like break dancing. We don't actually break anything."

He dropped, showing off some basic street dance moves he'd learned at his last school. This brought him a round of applause from the onlookers. Even Ms. Vartexia, who was slumped back in her seat looking a little ill, clapped politely.

The sillier and more outrageous John's dancing became, the more he impressed his classmates. While Great Red Spot bobbed on stage, John found himself at the center of a cheering circle.

"You didn't tell me you were such a great dancer," Emmie gasped, as the band finished their last song and floated away. "You could be a professional."

John grinned, certain she must be pulling his

leg, but as he looked into her navy-blue eyes he realized that the beautiful Sillaran was deadly serious.

"We Earthlings are naturally talented like that," he replied, trying not to burst out laughing again.

Emmie nodded enthusiastically. "Can you teach me some of those moves when we get back to Hyperspace High?"

John was about to agree, but just then, Ms. Vartexia interrupted.

"Time for bed," she said weakly. "Lots to do tomorrow."

The Hyperspace History teacher was swaying slightly and her blue skin had a greenish tinge.

"But it's still early," groaned Kaal. "I'm having a good time."

John shushed him. "If we keep her happy,

maybe she'll let us visit more interesting exhibits tomorrow," he said.

"I'm tired anyway," Emmie said with a yawn. "It's been a long day. I could definitely use some sleep."

The Shuttletube ride back to the space port passed quietly, except for Ms. Vartexia's frequent burps (and, of course, her embarrassed apologies).

Soon, John was back in his Privateer. At the touch of a button, the MorphSeat transformed itself into a comfortable bed. In a small locker, he found a light cover and pillow. A panel slid back at the rear of the ship to reveal a small sink and toilet.

As he began changing into his pajamas, John worried about the transparent shell of the ship. People could see him!

Then he remembered that from the outside,

the hull of the Privateer was opaque. What a relief.

After changing, John stretched out, feeling the MorphSeat warming beneath him.

"Not bad, huh?" Kaal's voice said through the intercom.

"Very comfy," John agreed.

"Okay. That reminds me of a Derrilian joke I heard once," Kaal said. "Two explorers are camping on a planet they've just discovered. One turns to the other and says, 'Can you hear something?' The other looks up and says, 'Only your feet.'"

There was a pause.

"Yes, and then what?" John asked. "What's next?"

"That's it. That's the joke."

"Oh, right —"

"Hahahaha!" John's answer was drowned

out by Emmie's hysterical laughter. "That's so funny. Do you want to hear a Sillaran gag?" she asked.

"Sure," John said.

"A Sillaran high priest visits a space station. At the entry port is a Vesuvian Burbeast. 'Hello,' says the high priest, 'there's a holy relic named after you.' The Burbeast looks at the priest and says, 'What: Jartex?'"

This time both Kaal and Emmie howled with laughter.

"W-w-why aren't you l-laughing, John?" Kaal finally managed to choke through his howls. "That's *hilarious*."

"Are Earth jokes as good as Earth dancing?" Emmie asked. "Tell us one."

"Yeah, let's hear an Earth joke," Kaal agreed.

"Okay," John replied. "Two cannibals are

eating a clown. One turns to the other and says, 'Does this taste funny to you?'"

There was a long silence.

"Still, at least Earthlings are good dancers," said Emmie with pity in her voice.

All three of them found this funnier than any of the jokes. It set off a giggling fit that lasted long after they should have been asleep.

Eventually, however, Emmie's yawns came more and more often and she finally dropped out of the conversation.

Before long, John heard the unmistakable grunts and horrible, loud grinding noises of his Derrilian roommate's snores. Quickly, he reached out and switched off the intercom.

Looking up through the transparent shell of the small spaceship, he watched the twin moons and stars of the alien sky.

All in all, he decided, it had been a pretty

good day. He had walked through a Martian dust storm and discovered a secret about the history of his own planet. The evening at Optical Orbit had been fantastic.

As his eyes closed, John wondered what fun the next day might bring.

CHAPTER 10

John frowned as Archivus Major's sun rose higher in the sky outside the window.

"Where *is* she?" he asked, looking around at his classmates. "Ms. Vartexia is *always* on time. It sends her into a twitching fit if she's even a *second* late."

As had been arranged the previous evening, the class had met at the space dock's Terrace Café for an early breakfast. That had been an hour ago. Everyone had eaten and was now eager to start the day's visits. Unfortunately, the Elvian teacher was nowhere to be seen.

"Maybe we should check on her," suggested Emmie. Impatient to leave the dock, the students agreed.

"Umm, *hello*. Are you in there?" Emmie called, rapping on the Privateer's shell.

No reply.

"*Ms. Vartexia!*" Emmie shouted, knocking again. "Is everything all right?"

"Do you think we should open the door?" asked John doubtfully. It seemed like a bad idea. Forcing their way into a teacher's private sleeping space seemed a good way to land a month's worth of detentions.

The students all looked at each other in silence.

"I think we should," said Emmie eventually. "She didn't look very well last night. Perhaps she's ill." Placing her hand on the craft, she said, "Emmie Tarz. Open up."

Nothing happened.

"Let me do it," said Kaal, pushing his way through the crowd. From his pocket he pulled a small device that he always carried around with him. It was called a ToTool, and John always thought of it as a sort of space-age Swiss army knife. At the flick of a switch, it seemed to be able to become whatever tool Kaal needed it to be.

Kaal aimed the ToTool at the side of the Privateer. A small beam of red light swept across the ship's glassy hull. Kaal grunted with satisfaction as a panel slid back, exposing delicate circuits. He flicked the ToTool again, and a needle-thin spike shot out. With steady hands, Kaal touched it to the circuitry.

"Computer: emergency override of privacy

protocols," he said. "Pilot Vartexia unable to respond and possibly in need of medical attention."

"Privacy protocols suspended," the computer voice replied.

John's eyebrows shot up in amazement at his friend's technical expertise, as the door panel of the Privateer slid back noiselessly. The students peered inside.

Wrapped in a cover, Ms. Vartexia's thin body was sprawled across the MorphSeat bed.

"Sleeping like a newborn Pataq grub," said Werril at the back of the small crowd.

"I'm not so sure," Emmie frowned. "She should have woken up by now." Reaching out, she shook the teacher's thin shoulder. "Ms. Vartexia. *Ms. Vartexia!*"

The Elvian didn't stir.

Emmie turned, her forehead lined with

worry. "There's something wrong with her," she said.

"Let me take a look," said Bareon, stepping forward. "My dad's a doctor with the Galactic Fleet."

John, Emmie, and Kaal stepped back to let him through.

Bareon leaned over. Placing a long-fingered hand on either side of Ms. Vartexia's neck, he said, "Both hearts beating slowly, but firmly." He lifted one of her eyelids. "Eyes look fine, and she's breathing without any problems. Werril's right, she's just sleeping." He stopped for a moment and then turned to face the students with a smile on his small mouth. "Of *course*, it must have been the Elvian spaghetti."

"What do you mean?" asked John. "Does she have food poisoning?"

"No," replied Bareon. "Elvian spaghetti

contains small amounts of sedative. Someone eating a normal portion would just feel relaxed after their meal, but in large quantities —"

"She had four huge bowls of it last night," Emmie chipped in.

"That's enough to keep her asleep until at least lunchtime," said Bareon. "You know, that seems a bit strange. She's Elvian, so she must have known what it would do to her to eat so much Elvian spaghetti."

"I remember the curator, Graximus Greyfore, telling her to try it," John said. "I guess he didn't know quite how much she'd like it." He paused for a moment, then added, "Is she going to be okay?"

"Oh, yes," Bareon said. "In fact, she'll wake up this afternoon feeling as fresh as a Coopit blossom."

"So what do we do now?" asked John,

voicing the question that everyone was thinking. "If there's nothing wrong with her, I don't want to hang around a space port for most of the day."

"I suppose someone ought to stay with her, just in case," said Bareon, sighing. "And since I'm the only one here with any medical knowledge, it'll have to be me. There's no need for the rest of you to stick around, though."

"Hmmm, I'm suddenly seeing an upside to this," said John, a smile spreading across his face. "No Ms. Vartexia means no rocks, no moss gardens, no stupid art galleries . . . "

Kaal already had his ThinScreen guide out. "Okay," he said with a grin. "Let's vote on what to see first."

Emmie turned toward them, with a matching look of delight on her face. "There's more good news," she said happily. "I checked out the Information Center while we were waiting, and they have Space-Stilts. Ms. Vartexia would never have let us use them, but, you know, if she's asleep . . . " She shrugged as her voice trailed off.

"She never needs to know," Lishtig finished for her, with a chuckle.

"Space-Stilts?" asked John.

"I cannot wait to see your face when you try them," said Emmie.

* * *

"So tell me again, what do these do?" asked John, as he pulled on a pair of heavy boots. Extending out from the heels were lengths of curved metal.

"They act like springs," explained Kaal. "So you can jump across long distances quickly."

"Are you sure they're not dangerous?" John asked, looking at his friend nervously. "I noticed you're not wearing any."

"Hello? *Wings?*" Kaal replied, rustling them. "Some of us don't need gadgets."

"You'll be fine, John," Emmie interrupted. "They have all kinds of built-in safety features. You just turn them on here." She pointed at buttons on the back of the boots. "No, not *NOW!*" she yelled. "Don't turn them on in *here*, you'll splat yourself on the ceiling. Wait until we're outside."

Leaning heavily on Kaal's shoulder, John tottered through the door, feeling like a newborn giraffe.

"*Now* you can turn them on."

Flicking buttons on each boot, John was amazed to find that he was immediately more stable.

The Space-Stilts hummed. Nervously, he stood as still as possible.

"First, we're going to the jungle," said Queelin smugly. Emmie, of course, had wanted to go to the frozen Goran-Subo battlefield right away, but she had been outvoted.

Turning to John, Emmie explained, "You just need to do *this*."

Emmie bounced once on a heel and shot elegantly into the sky with a whoop. In a single bound, she leaped across buildings, landing almost a mile away and instantly bouncing into the sky again.

"Yee-*hah*!" yelled Lishtig, following her. "Last one there's a Skantard."

As the students bounded after Emmie, shrieking with laughter, John tried a small experimental hop. "Waaaah!" he cried, flailing his arms as he shot high in the air.

"You'll get the hang of it," said Kaal, as his friend finally bounced to a stop. "Come on, I'll keep you company."

"This is *amazing*!" called John, as he leaped into the air again.

"You should try wings!" Kaal yelled back, swooping through the air alongside him.

John didn't reply. The ground was coming up fast. Putting a foot forward, he felt an enormous surge as energies were released, then he was climbing high into the air again.

Bet they don't do this at Wortham Court, he thought.

Emmie had been right: the Space-Stilts were easy to master. After just a few leaps, John felt like he had been using them all his life. And sailing through the air with the breeze whipping his hair back was much more fun than taking the Shuttletube.

"Stop on the next leap!" shouted Kaal, diving past, wings outstretched. "By the Information Center."

"Stop? How do I . . . *Gaaaahh!*"

CRASH!

John smashed into a clump of thick undergrowth. He lay there without moving. A low moan escaped his lips.

"Nice landing, John," said Lishtig, lifting his purple eyebrows.

"Hey, it's my first time," John replied, pulling twigs from his hair.

The rest of the class had already removed their Space-Stilts. They were waiting by the Teride Six Jungle Environment as John and Lishtig trotted down a path overhung by a dense canopy of purple leaves.

Queelin Temerate was pointing to a large map. "If we walk along the pathway there," she was saying, "we might see Flurbs and Sinches, plus we'll end up at a simulation of the Great Teride Falls." Catching sight of John, she broke off and grinned at him. "Anyone tell you what a great landing that was?" she asked.

"Yes. Lishtig. Thanks, Queelin."

Walking beneath the branches of an alien jungle was a mind-boggling experience. The trees alone were like nothing John had ever seen before. Some had trunks the thickness of a house and were twisted around with snake-like vines; others were covered in flowers the size of trash-can lids and smelled powerfully of oranges.

Between the trees were scattered the leaf-thatched longhouses the Teridean people had lived in millions of years ago. Insects larger than parrots, and more brightly colored, hovered in the dappled sunlight.

The calls of larger beasts sounded in the

distance and, beyond, was the unmistakable roar of a waterfall.

"John," whispered Emmie, after they had walked about a mile. "Don't move. There's a Flurb, just to your left."

"A what?"

"A Flurb. *Shhhh.*"

Standing as still as possible, John turned his head slowly. About a yard from his feet, half hidden in a bush, was an animal that looked like a cross between a monkey and a large hamster, except that it had six legs.

"Awww," John whispered. "Look at its little face." Slowly, he dropped to his knees.

"Uh, John. I'm not sure that's a good idea," Emmie whispered nervously, as he stretched his hand out to pet the Flurb.

"Don't be silly. Look how cute it is."

Click.

Metal fingers closed around his wrist, moving it back just as the Flurb bared a hideous set of razor-sharp fangs. As the creature's prey was jerked away, it turned and scampered into the bushes.

"Aaaargh, no!" bellowed Kaal, covering his ears. "Here comes that alarm again."

Blinking in shock, John gazed at the metal fingers restraining him, trailed up the metal arm, and then looked up into the steady electronic eyes of an Omega-bot.

This time, no alarm went off. "Do not touch the exhibits," the machine droned, dropping John's hand.

"S-sorry," John stammered. Over the past twenty-four hours he had become so used to the machines following them everywhere that he had completely forgotten about them. Remembering the nasty look on the Flurb's face, he suddenly felt grateful for their presence. "Um, thanks," he added.

"Do not touch the exhibits," the Omega-bot repeated blankly. Then it turned and floated away.

"Sheesh, they're like Examiners with firepower," said John, as Emmie and Kaal hurried over.

"Yeah, and ear-melting sirens," Kaal added.

"Two very good reasons to not upset them. Come on, let's get to the waterfall," Emmie replied, pushing them forward.

The falls were spectacular.

Almost a hundred different streams crashed over rocks into a lake of clear orange water. Rainbows hung in the air.

"Can we swim?" asked John, looking at the cool water longingly.

"You could," Kaal replied, checking his

ThinScreen guide. "But it says here the lake contains Pain Snakes."

"They don't sound good."

"Apparently, it's not a very accurate name," Kaal continued. "If they bite you, the venom causes hardly any pain at all. Just immediate death."

"Great. How about we move on to the next exhibit?"

As the morning passed, it was as if Archivus Major was making up for the disappointments of the day before. Crossing vast distances in huge strides with the help of the Space-Stilts — and using the Shuttletube only when it would have taken too long to bounce — the class visited the most interesting displays the planet had to offer. Emmie and Queelin loved the Floating Pleasure Gardens of Vox Charm, and even Kaal grumpily agreed that the Silken Desert Palace of Queen Alaria was breathtakingly lovely. John was flabbergasted by the Star Dragon skeleton. The creature's head alone was the size of a cruise ship. Sparkling like cut diamonds, its crystal bones stretched as far as his eyes could see.

"The only living creatures that have ever managed to live in the hard vacuum of space," said Kaal, ThinScreen guide in hand. "No one knows where they came from or where they went, but the Star Dragons disappeared about twenty million years ago. According to this, they starved for thousands of years as they flew between planets. Then, when they found one, they devoured everything on the surface."

"Uh . . . so they might come back?" asked John, trying not to imagine the scenes of devastation if a Star Dragon ever descended on Earth.

Kaal switched off his ThinScreen. "Maybe," he said, shrugging. "No one knows."

"Come on, everyone!" called Emmie impatiently. "We've done what you wanted to do. Now can we *please* go to the battlefield?"

CHAPTER 11

Getting to the battlefield exhibit meant a half-hour ride across the planet. It was almost lunchtime when the Shuttletube swept into the station, but Emmie was far too excited to think about eating.

"We'll just see *some* of it," she said happily as the class streamed through the Shuttletube exit, "and stop for lunch after that. Then we'll have time for a better look. John . . . *John*. Hurry up." She had pulled the Comet Creative from her bag and was already running forward. "Got to find the best place to get a picture!" she shouted over her shoulder.

John and Kaal glanced at each other, frowning. Hyperspace History was one of Emmie's worst subjects, and she had never showed the slightest interest in the Goran-Subo war before Graximus Greyfore had talked to them about it.

However, Emmie's unusual behavior was quickly forgotten. As they cleared the exit, both John and Kaal stopped in their tracks. Before them was a vast block of crystal-clear ice and inside was nothing less than a complete battle, frozen in time.

The entire class had fallen silent. There was no laughter or happy chatter now. Every eye, antenna, and sight-sensor was turned to the towering ice block.

In front of them, across a dreary landscape of mud and bogs, the creatures John had seen in the 4-D movie at Hyperspace High were locked in close combat.

The Goran — looking like heavily armored tanks with great pincers — against the blubbery Subo, seal-like, except for the long laser spikes jutting from their heads.

Spikes that could be used to stab their enemies.

Several Subo had been frozen in exactly such a pose.

"Come on, there's tons more to see." Emmie clapped her hands to attract attention and pointed the students to a path around the exhibit. "Over there looks like a good place to take a 4-D photo."

As the rest of the class moved away, John stopped by an information screen. It immediately changed, as the characters on its screen transformed to English. Fascinated, he leaned in to read.

"Over two hundred thousand warriors, including Suboran's infamous General Klort, are held inside this stasis cube. It is the largest display of suspension technology in the history of the galaxy," the screen told him. "It was developed in complete secrecy, at a time when ninety-five percent of space-faring civilizations were at war."

Shaking his head in amazement, John continued reading the story of how the frozen battle had come to rest on Archivus Major. At the height of the war, members of the Galactic Council had formed a top-secret peace group. Hiding deep within a gigantic hollow asteroid, they created factories that produced immense spaceships — *Peace Stars 1, 2, 3, 4,* and *5.*

Each spaceship was equipped with powerful suspension beams.

Escorted by a fleet of smaller fighter craft, the *Peace Stars* had battled their way through space to the center of the Goran-Subo war. There, they had released the power of their beams. With the warmonger, General Klort — as well as top generals on both sides — in stasis, the Subo and Goran governments had quickly laid down arms and, under threat of suspension from the Council, the rest of the galaxy soon followed.

"With the war over," the screen finished, "it was decided that releasing the fighters from suspension was too great a threat to the new-found peace. Instead, the *Peace Stars* cut the entire battlefield from Gora Prime's surface and towed it to Archivus Major. It now serves as a reminder of the horror of war. By order of the

Galactic Council, the warriors within will never be released."

"They're all still alive in there," Kaal's voice said, breaking through John's thoughts. "Just held in suspended animation for thirty thousand years."

Lost for words, John looked up at his friend, nodded, and then returned his gaze to the scene within the stasis cube.

A thick line of heavily armored Goran were frozen in the act of charging a weaker line of Subo: thousands of fighters' screaming battle cries that had been silenced forever. Even explosions had been caught by the stasis beams. Like great flowers of yellow and orange, they dotted the landscape, throwing giant sprays of earth into the air.

"We're getting left behind," said Kaal, pointing to the rest of the class. The other students were now some distance away. "Better catch up or they'll lose us."

"What do you think, John?" asked Emmie excitedly, as John and Kaal joined the group. "It's spooky, isn't it? And sad, too."

"Yeah," John agreed quickly. "But it really makes you think, doesn't it? If every Hyperspace History class were like this, I'd be getting the best grades in the class."

"Speaking of grades," Emmie said, "where's a good place to use the Comet Creative? I want to get the best view." She held up the device. To John, it looked just like a very large digital camera.

"Okay, Emmie," said Kaal. "Let's get it over with and then maybe you'll calm down."

John's forehead tensed in worry. Something Emmie had said was niggling at the back of his mind.

Emmie, however, was dancing from one foot to the other in eagerness. "Hey, with the extra credit that Graximus Greyfore is going to give me, maybe this term I won't be bottom of the class," she said, grinning.

Extra credit, thought John. *Something about the extra credit doesn't add up.*

Emmie was still gibbering. "I think I should get a picture of you standing in front of it first, Kaal. You can send it to your dad."

"Great idea," said Kaal enthusiastically. "He's really interested to see what a human being looks like, too, so John should be in it. Let's find somewhere with a really impressive background. Lots of action, that's what we need."

As Emmie and Kaal hurried along the path, John followed more slowly, lost in thought. Unable to put his finger on what was bothering him, he decided he was being ridiculous and picked up his pace.

"Perfect," said Kaal, pointing to a particular scene in the stasis cube. A lone Goran raising a tattered, mud-streaked flag reared up defiantly as a wave of Subo fell upon it. "John, come and stand over here."

John hurried over and took position next to his friend, smiling as Kaal put an arm around his shoulders.

"Ready!" the Derrilian shouted.

"Wonder how many extra marks I'm going to get for this," said Emmie, pointing the Comet Creative and looking through the viewfinder. "Looks good, guys. Smile."

Of course, that's what's wrong. Realization hit John at the same time as Emmie hit the activate button.

Graximus Greyfore had promised Emmie

extra credit, but told her to keep the Comet Creative a secret. Greyfore wasn't a teacher, so how was Emmie going to get extra credit if no one could find out about it?

"Wait!" John shouted. Farther up the path, students turned to look, surprised by the urgency in his voice.

Too late.

John raised his arm across his eyes, as the Comet Creative gave off a blinding flash that lit the sky.

"What the —" Still clutching the Comet Creative, Emmie staggered, covering her face with her free hand to protect her own eyes. As the flash faded, she screamed.

Two Omega-bots were bearing down on her at top speed. "It's okay!" she yelled desperately. "Graximus Greyfore gave it to me. The curator. *Graximus Greyfore* told me to use it!"

The Omega-bots ignored her. Metal claws gripped her by the arms.

"Hey, leave her alone!" John shouted, trying to shove the nearest Omega-bot away from Emmie. "Didn't you hear her? Greyfore said it was okay."

Deep down, however, he knew that something was seriously amiss. If the Comet Creative was such a great new invention, why didn't Greyfore want to test it himself? Why give it to a visiting student?

Behind him, John heard a shout in a language he was coming to recognize as Derrilian. As Archivus Major's computer systems hadn't translated it, he knew his friend must have sworn.

Snapping his head around, John saw Kaal backing toward him, one arm raised in alarm. John followed his friend's pointing finger.

After 30,000 years, the stasis cube was melting.

CHAPTER 12

High above, water poured down the sides of the stasis cube. As the ice melted, students goggled. A small flood, bigger with every passing second, began gurgling around their feet.

"What did you *do*, Tarz?" Lishtig whispered in disbelief.

Emmie didn't answer. Her face was gray, her navy-blue eyes fixed, unblinking, on the scene before her.

John, too, was unable to take his eyes off the

exhibit. The Omega-bots forgotten, he stared as streams of water turned into a continuous rushing fall along the entire length of the stasis cube.

Somewhere in the distance an alarm blared. With a clash of metal, the Omega-bots' claws released Emmie's arm. The two machines moved to take new positions farther back from the cube, a short distance from each other. Neither gave any instructions to the students around them.

Still staring wildly, Emmie walked toward the ice, hand stretched out to touch the gushing water.

"No," she whispered. "This can't be happening."

A few feet from her, Kaal hadn't moved since his warning shout. Like the rest of the class, he seemed to be rooted to the spot.

Water rushed past John's ankles, threatening to knock him off his feet. He heard a long, blood-chilling shriek that drowned out the sirens in the distance.

What's going on? he wondered.

Another scream rang out, followed by the sounds of blasts and explosions.

It was a battle cry.

The stasis cube was now less than three-quarters of its original height.

John gasped as freezing water passed his knees. A split second later, he forgot all about the cold: the scene before his eyes was much more chilling.

As they emerged from the ice, the Goran and Subo warriors that had been on the highest ground were now resuming their fight exactly where they had left off.

Most of the soldiers in the bogs below were

still trapped but, as John watched, a Goran lunged at the closest Subo.

"Die, Subo!" it howled in triumph. The Subo thrashed its supple body, desperate to escape the ice.

It failed. Caught in the Goran's pincers, massive wounds opened up along its neck. The enraged Subo twisted in the Goran's grip, screaming as its laser-horn flickered to life.

A jet of light flashed. The Goran howled as one of its pincers was lopped from its body. The Subo was now free of the ice and able to slither toward its enemy. It closed in for a fresh attack, shrieking.

The cube was now half melted. Water gurgled and swirled around John's thighs. Jagged blocks of ice swept past.

Across the melting ice, thousands of warriors were coming to life. In the distance, John could see a hill that looked like a command post. He heard a roaring voice giving commands, massively amplified so that every soldier could hear.

"This is General Klort, Commander of the Subo forces. Attack the Goran. Show them no mercy. Kill them. *Kill them all!*"

A great cheer swelled in the Subo ranks. As if answering their general, devastating charges that had been frozen on high ground for thousands of years began to fall once again upon enemy ranks below. Subo and Goran slid across the ice in killing lust. Explosions burst into life again, splattering the scene with great gobs of mud and broken bodies.

As the ice melted, the roar of battle became deafening. Somewhere, the alarm was still sounding, but John could barely hear it. He watched, fascinated, as lines of laser fire were exchanged for bullets and exploding bombs. Giant pincers met the deadly points of laser-horns.

Here, a Subo went down, squealing under a tank-like Goran, never to get up again. There, a Goran howled its last as it was cut to pieces by laser fire.

John's eyes moved across the scene. Neither side seemed to be winning. In one place, a Goran line collapsed under the weight of attacking Subo in one place.

For a moment, John thought that might give them the advantage. Then, just mere seconds later, the same happened to a line of Subo soldiers.

There was no order to the chaos: General Klort roared orders, but most of her troops were too bogged down to respond. The entire battle was one vast, bloodthirsty brawl. Kill or be killed. Horrifying in its violence, but at the same time mesmerizing.

"*John.* Get out of there!"

Lishtig splashed past him, through water mixed with battlefield mud. Beside him, Queelin Temerate slipped and fell. Lishtig caught her by the arm.

Half crawling, half dragging each other, the two students moved away toward the Omega-bots. The students were fleeing.

John heard a whining noise fifty feet to his right. Suddenly, an explosion flung him onto his knees. Choking on the icy mud, he lifted his head as realization flooded through him. This wasn't a 4-D movie or one of Archivus Major's amazing replicas.

It was a war.

And it was happening right in front of him.

Most of his classmates had made it to dry

ground past the Omega-bots that had restrained Emmie only a few minutes before.

Now, more of the great droids were arriving — hundreds of them buzzed through the air and clanked to a halt in a line at the edge of the battlefield. Quickly, a ring of Omega-bots was forming around the entire exhibit.

John took a step toward the metal guardians of Archivus Major and then stopped. Kaal and Emmie were still standing where he had last seen them, right next to the melting stasis cube. The battle was raging just feet from where they stood. Water was halfway up Emmie's thighs and as high as Kaal's knees.

John could see Emmie's gaped mouth as she tried to make sense of what she was seeing, what she had done. Kaal was simply staring, lost in the action unfolding.

The words of Graximus Greyfore suddenly

came back to John: "We will never know how the battle would have ended."

"Wanna bet?" he muttered to himself as he stepped through the sludge.

"*KAAAAAL!*" he yelled at the top of his lungs, fear giving his voice an urgency that caught the Derrilian's attention, even through the noise of battle.

Kaal turned. Wading more quickly now, John pointed toward Emmie.

Suddenly, Kaal became aware of the danger they were in. Shaking his head, he unfurled his wings, flapping them to help drive him through the muddy water.

They arrived at Emmie at the same time, each reaching out to pull her away.

Eyes fixed on the fight, she struggled against her friends. "My fault," she whispered. "This is all *my* fault."

"No, it's not!" John yelled. "Come on, we've got to get away from here."

Emmie turned toward him, her face streaked with mud and tears.

"It's not your fault, Emmie," John repeated as gently as he could with the battle raging a few yards away. "Just run for it. *Please.*"

"Let's go, Tarz. That's an order!" Kaal shouted. This time, she didn't struggle. Glancing over her shoulder in horror, she allowed them to drag her over the drenched ground.

"Quickly," panted John, as they waded through the cold gloop. "The Omega-bots can handle this." They were close now, the water shallower as they clambered up a low hill. "Just a few more steps, Emmie."

With a last effort, the three friends hurled themselves toward a gap in the line of metal droids.

Suddenly, there was a fizzing noise and a surge of energy.

Together, they were thrown back.

"What on Earth —" John began. Catching hold of Emmie's arm once more, he threw himself forward.

And again, a charge of energy threw him back. "Aarrgghhh!" he screamed.

"It's a force field!" Kaal shouted. "The Omega-bots are acting like fence posts in a ring of force surrounding the battlefield."

John looked up. On each side of the Omega-bots' heads, green eyes glowed with power. He put his hand out and yanked it back quickly, his fingertips smarting.

Kaal was right. There was an invisible wall between the tall robots.

John waded over to the closest robot and slammed his fist against its metal casing. "Hey, you!" he yelled. "We're trapped in here. Let us out."

The Omega-bot remained perfectly still, and perfectly silent.

"I said —"

"It's no use, John."

John looked back to see Kaal pushing against the force field. It hadn't budged.

"But they're supposed to be protecting us," John said.

"No, they're not," Emmie cut in, her voice thick with misery. "They're supposed to protect the exhibits, and that's exactly what they're doing. They won't let anything out." She paused for a moment, then held out the Comet Creative. "I'm sorry, this is all my fault. I must have pressed the wrong button."

"It wasn't you, Emmie," John replied. "I realized Greyfore must have been up to something just as you pressed the button. Why did he want to keep the Comet Creative a secret? Why give it to a student at all? Looks to me like he planned this. I think he *wanted* it to happen."

Emmie looked up at him hopefully. "You mean it wasn't —"

"I hate to interrupt, but just to remind you, we're kind of fenced in with two hundred thousand warriors," Kaal interrupted. "Pretty soon, one of them is going to wonder why they just woke up in a block of ice on a different planet."

"Good point." John waved his arms, standing as close to the invisible barrier as he dared.

On the other side of the field, Lishtig's head turned. John saw his mouth moving, but no sound made it through the invisible barrier between them. The purple-haired student turned back to his classmates, apparently shouting. A few moments later they were running toward their side of the barrier. Lishtig arrived first and began banging his fists against it. When that failed, he, too, tried to attract an Omega-bot's attention.

"It's no good, they're programmed to contain any disaster," Kaal said, panting. "The Omega-bots will maintain the force field for as long as they can."

"So, we're stuck in here?" John tried to keep the terror he felt from his voice.

Kaal nodded. "Unless we can either fix the battlefield or disable the Omega-bots."

John glanced at the battle. It had taken five specially built *Peace Stars* to freeze it 30,000 years ago.

He returned his gaze to the unmoving line of Omega-bots. Each was heavily armed and built to fight off anyone or anything trying to interfere with Archivus Major's exhibits.

John's shoulders sagged in defeat. "There's no hope, then?"

"There's always hope. Emmie, give me the Comet Creative."

Emmie didn't reply. Standing stock-still, she stared ahead of her.

John and Kaal followed her gaze.

From the corner of his eye, John saw his classmates beating against the force field with even more urgency. He didn't move, didn't even breathe.

A massive Subo warrior had fallen from the ice and was staring at them with its dark, beady eyes. It looked along the line of Omega-bots, then lifted its head to gaze at the sky above. With a snort of angry confusion, it looked back at the three beings who had no business on a Goran-Subo battlefield.

"Who are you? What is this place?" it snarled.

The Subo lowered its laser-horn and began moving forward on short, flipper-like hind legs. John looked around desperately, but there was nowhere to go.

The Subo opened its mouth. "This is Goran trickery. You are enemies of the Subo race," it growled. "All enemies must die."

CHAPTER 13

The Subo reared up, preparing to charge the three students.

Suddenly, a laser beam exploded from the Subo's deadly horn. John tried to leap out of the way, but the laser caught his sleeve. Before John had a chance to recover, another battle cry filled the air.

Kaal shrieked as he tore past his friends in a blur of frantically beating wings.

"Kaal, *NO*! It'll kill you!" Emmie yelled.

The Derrilian ignored Emmie's terrified shout. Diving to avoid the Subo's laser-horn, he closed in on the beast, his yell mixing with the howling of the alien warrior.

Kaal hit just below its bulbous head, where its thick neck widened into powerful shoulders. The force of the blow toppled the Subo. Its massive bulk fell into the water, a muddy wave drenching John and Emmie.

Kaal dived on the Subo like a hawk attacking its prey. Wrapping strong arms around its neck, he sank his sharp fangs into the Subo's blubbery flesh.

A howl of pain ripped through the air. Bucking and thrashing beneath him, the Subo tried to bring its horn round to stab its attacker. The laser began firing randomly, bursts of burning light slamming into the force field wall close to John and Emmie.

"Get down!" Emmie commanded, pulling John into the mud.

Another flash of laser fire hit an Omega-bot behind them. The droid cracked and fizzled, its metal casing spitting sparks. The energy wall flickered and then stabilized again.

The Subo was bigger and heavier than Kaal, but the tall, heavily muscled Derrilian was much faster and his thick, green arms were strong. He also had the advantage of flight. Every time the Subo lunged at him, Kaal flew beyond the warrior's reach and then dived back to attack again.

With a grunt of effort, Kaal grabbed the Subo's laser-horn with one hand and clamped his legs around the warrior's back. Lying in the mud, John watched helplessly as his friend grappled with the warrior, his face showing the strain.

There was a sharp crack and a spray of sparks. The laser-horn snapped. Shouting in triumph, Kaal raised it high and plunged the deadly tip into the Subo's flesh.

A hideous screech of rage filled the air. "I'll tear you apart!" raged the Subo. Screaming in agony, it erupted beneath the Derrilian, thrashing to rid itself of its rider.

Kaal was forced to leap away before he was crushed beneath the Subo's weight, but the warrior's head smashed into Kaal's stomach as he jumped.

John gasped as Kaal was thrown into the water. His friend fell forward, face down into the swirling, frozen lake.

The Subo's scream of pain turned to one of conquest as it saw its enemy helpless. Twisting its bulk around, it reared once again.

"No you don't, you ugly freak."

A large chunk of ice smashed into the Subo's head just above its eyes.

"He shoots, he scores!" John shouted wildly, desperate to keep the Subo's attention away from the motionless Kaal. Reaching down, his fingers found another block of ice. He threw it with all his strength, dancing from one foot to another as it shattered against the creature's snout.

With Kaal forgotten, the Subo turned its bulk toward John. "Tiny creature," it said, sneering. "You won't last ten seconds against one of General Klort's elite warriors."

Despite its tough words, John noticed that the Subo was moving slower now, black blood pumping from the wound in its shoulder where Kaal had stabbed it. Roaring a battle cry, the beast charged at him.

"Think you can take both of us?" Another

chunk of ice hurtled through the air, smacking into the Subo's blubbery neck. Following John's lead, Emmie was throwing whatever she could lay her hands on.

Confused, the creature's head weaved from side to side, trying to watch both its new enemies at once as they waded toward it, hurling lumps of ice and rock.

The Subo threw itself toward John, forcing him to stagger backward until his back was almost against the force field. Seeing the danger, Emmie renewed her attack. Her missiles bounced off the Subo's skin. Still it charged, straight toward John.

"Don't worry about me, help Kaal!" John yelled at Emmie. He looked in the mud for something, anything, to throw.

The Subo dodged as John rained chunks of ice upon it with all his strength. John's fingers were throbbing with cold, his strength dwindling, but by aiming at the creature's tiny eyes and keeping up a constant barrage, he managed to hold off the Subo. Behind it, he saw Emmie shaking Kaal back to consciousness and dragging the Derrilian to his feet.

"Kaal, take Emmie. *Fly!*" he yelled, slipping on the mud.

Seeing John fall, the Subo again charged forward. "Now you are *mine!*" it bellowed, its great bulk cutting off John's view of his friends.

John tried to wriggle backward, one hand searching for something else to throw. His fingers closed around a small rock.

Panic rising, John flung his arm back, taking aim. Just then, Kaal hit the Subo like a green comet, pounding a fist into its head.

Still clutching his rock, John ran toward Emmie, eyes widening in shock as he realized the stasis cube had now melted completely. Every warrior was free, the combat more intense than ever.

"Cut them down, soldiers of Suboran!" screeched General Klort. "Cut them down and history will never forget your names."

Soldiers were spreading toward them. With a sinking heart, John realized that they might, possibly, be able to defeat one Subo between the three of them, but within a few minutes hundreds of Subo — and Goran too — would be right on top of them.

He looked back. The Omega-bots hadn't moved an inch.

There's nothing we can do.

John's fingers tightened around the rock, preparing to rejoin the fight. Its shape jogged something in the back of his mind. Whatever he was holding wasn't a rock.

Glancing down, he wiped away some mud.

The Comet Creative.

Emmie must have dropped it when she attacked the Subo.

John stared at the technology in his hand, his brain whirring. The small machine had caused this disaster. Perhaps it could fix it too. His own knowledge of advanced technology was pitiful, but Kaal spent many evenings in their dorm room tinkering with whatever bits of technology he could lay his hands on.

John knew what he had to do. Through knee-deep water, he quickly waded back toward the Subo.

The creature was standing on stubby back flippers, snaking from side to side as it tried to land a blow on Kaal. The Derrilian was swooping about its head, lashing out with his fists and feet whenever he saw a chance.

When John reached the Subo, he leaped from the ground, aiming a flying kick at the warrior from behind.

The creature whirled. "You were lucky before!" it screamed, spotting John. "But not this time."

"What are you doing? I'm okay. Get out of here!" Kaal yelled as the creature shifted its bulk to attack John again. Its movements were much slower now, but the huge creature was still dangerous.

"I can take care of it!" John yelled back. "See if you can do anything with this."

The Comet Creative spun through the air. With a flurry of wings, Kaal dived sideways and snatched it. John was already stumbling backward through the water, tossing more chunks of ice and rock at the Subo.

"You call yourself an elite warrior?"

he shouted. "I've seen better fighters on kindergarten playgrounds."

With a grunt, the Subo summoned what was left of its strength, charging John with unexpected speed.

John looked up into a massive jaw edged with knife-like teeth. Dropping to the ground and rolling away, John splashed through water and jumped back onto his feet by the Subo's side, reaching out for the laser-horn that was still sticking out of the warrior's skin. With a fleshy, sucking noise, it came free, making the Subo scream in pain. Black blood spattered across John's face.

The Subo writhed in pain. John risked a glance toward Kaal. Close to the Omega-bot barrier where the water was more shallow, the Derrilian worked on the Comet Creative with his ToTool.

Raising his new weapon, John prepared to throw himself at the Subo again.

"John! Be careful!" A rock hurtled through the air. Emmie. It missed the Subo and clattered behind John.

She's got a great throwing arm, but really bad aim.

The thought was interrupted by a low snarl. Heart frozen, John spun around. A Goran was staring at him through one great eye in the middle of its shell. Between huge pincers it held the rock Emmie had thrown.

For a single moment everything was still. Then the Goran opened its pincers, letting the rock fall into the water that swirled around its short, heavily armored legs. "You are not a part of the Goran army, small alien," it said. "Therefore, you must be with the Subo. You are my enemy."

At the same time, John heard a roar behind

him. He spun around again. Blood dripping from its wound, the Subo glared at him with hatred in its eyes. It seemed so intent on revenge against John that it had forgotten its original enemy.

John looked from one alien to another.

"*RUN*, JOHN!" Emmie screamed.

The sound drove both creatures into action. The ground beneath John's feet rumbled as they rushed toward him.

Running was useless. John was caught between two terrifying aliens, his only weapon a broken laser-horn.

Emmie shouted again, her voice cracking with a sob of fear.

Neither alien took any notice. Both were focused on their prey. They knew it could not escape.

John squared his shoulders.

Might as well go down fighting, he thought.

Trapped between the oncoming warriors, he brandished the laser-horn in the air. On one side, the Subo reared up again; on the other, the Goran's huge pincers reached out to tear him apart.

John stood his ground. "Come on!" he yelled at the top of his lungs.

The Goran was closer. Leaving himself open to attack from the Subo on the opposite side, John swung the laser-horn with all his might. It smashed into the alien beast's pincer with a sharp crunching noise. The tip of its claw snapped off and flew into the mud.

John yelled in jubilation as the creature shrieked in pain.

His moment of triumph was short-lived. One pincer was damaged but the Goran had plenty more. It leaped at John, claws clacking in fury. At the same time the Subo fell upon him, its mouth roaring for revenge. It was so near, John could smell its foul breath.

He tried swinging his weapon again. It was no good — the aliens were right on top of him. Instinctively, he ducked and squeezed his eyes closed as a giant claw thrust at him. The shrieking Subo snapped at his head.

John steeled himself for what was to come. He hoped it would be quick.

This is it.

CHAPTER 14

Time seemed to slow down. A thousand memories chased through John's mind. Thoughts of his parents and friends, home: all the things he would never see again.

The moment seemed to stretch.

John had heard before that people in terrible danger often reported later that their entire lives had flashed before their eyes. He hadn't expected that the experience would take so long, though.

He clenched his teeth, waiting for the mauling he was sure would begin at any moment.

"John! John! Are you all right?" It was Emmie's voice, shouting from a distance.

An unbelievable sight met his eyes as they blinked open: the Goran and Subo were moving backward.

Adrenalin surged through him. Surely the beasts were only readying themselves for a fresh attack.

"*Cowards!*" he yelled, swinging the laser-horn. "Come on, let's finish this."

Still, the creatures moved away. John frowned. There was something odd about their movements. The way they were backing off looked like someone had pressed rewind on an old video player.

Kaal landed by his side. "It's okay," the Derrilian said gently, dodging to avoid the weapon John was still whipping around dangerously. "You can put that down now. I think I fixed it."

"W-what?" John stared at his friend, unable to grasp what he was hearing. Every part of him was ready for a fight to the death: *his* death.

"Please," the big Derrilian said, "drop it. Seriously, before you take someone's eye out or something."

Unwilling to let go of his only weapon, John's fingers stayed clenched around it, though he stopped waving it around.

"Wait a second. What are you saying?" John demanded.

Emmie waded over to join them. "It's over," she panted. "Kaal did it. Thanks to you." She flung her arms around him, sobbing. "I thought you were going to die."

At last, John dropped the laser-horn.

Returning Emmie's fierce hug, he looked over her head at Kaal. "I-I d-don't understand," he stammered.

"Look around," Kaal said.

John turned his head.

The Goran had backed into the battle and now appeared to be bringing a Subo back to life. As its pincers touched the Subo, its enemy's wounds closed. The Subo looked healthier with every moment and was now thrashing wildly. Bursts of light erupted from blackened holes in the Goran's shell and disappeared back into the tip of its laser-horn, leaving the Goran untouched.

John looked the other way.

The Subo that had attacked them seemed to be performing some kind of dance. John watched as it flopped backward through the mud. It turned, roaring at the place by the Omega-bots' force field where John had been standing a few moments earlier, then continued its backward shuffle. It was still for a moment, then reared up, snapping at an invisible opponent.

Behind the force field, John could see Hyperspace High students leaping in the air with joy.

John glanced down.

Water, too, was flowing in reverse. His eyes followed it. The stasis cube was beginning to reform. Subo and Goran were skittering backward across the ice, lines of warriors hurling themselves away from one another to take up their original positions.

Explosions became implosions, fiery blossoms closing with a strange roar that was suddenly silenced.

"How?" John asked.

Kaal held up the Comet Creative. "Simple,"

he said. "Although not *that* simple, even if I say so myself. At first I thought the device must be an anti-stasis emitter that reverses the polarity of the suspension particles at a quantum level, but it turns out that actually, it's more sophisticated than that. It sends out a highly charged temporal field that attaches itself to anything with a stasis signature. . . . "

John listened as Kaal reeled off technical information that meant nothing to him. "Any chance you can repeat all that in words I might actually understand?" he cut in when the Derrilian took a breath.

Kaal grinned. "The Comet Creative created a time field that took the stasis cube and everything in it back to a moment just before it was created, thirty thousand years ago," he explained. "Whoever made it disabled the function that would allow it to be reversed.

Once I knew what it was, it was a pretty easy repair job."

"*Pretty easy?*" John gaped. "A *pretty easy* repair job? Where did you learn to do something like that?"

"Hyperspace High *is* the best school in the galaxy," Kaal said, shrugging.

"So how come we're not going backward too?" asked Emmie, watching in fascination as water ran up the sides of the stasis cube. It was quieter now. Only a few Goran and Subo were making their reverse battle cries. The rest had disappeared under ice. The water was rapidly disappearing.

"We weren't in the cube," Kaal replied. "The field only interfered with anything that was originally held in stasis."

"I'm not sure I understand," John said, shaking his head.

Kaal slapped him on the shoulder. "Well," he said, grinning. "If you didn't fall asleep in classes all the time, you'd —"

He didn't make it to the end of the sentence. The three friends were suddenly mobbed by the rest of the class.

"Chang-do's Holy Bath Tub! Are you guys all right?" yelled Lishtig. "I thought you were goners for sure."

"That Goran had its claws right round your neck, John," Werril bellowed in his ear. "Right round your *neck*. I couldn't even look."

"You were *brilliant*," Queelin shouted over the yells of relief and congratulations. "The way you took on both of those horrible things? That was so —"

"Hey, it was Kaal who fixed everything," John interrupted.

"Well, I wouldn't have been able to fix

anything if Emmie hadn't rescued me from the water," Kaal replied, looking embarrassed.

A loud electronic voice interrupted the excitement. "Visit terminated. Return to the space dock and leave the planet immediately."

The class looked around. They were surrounded by Omega-bots.

John broke the silence. After the terrors he had just experienced, the menacing droids of Archivus Major didn't seem all that frightening. "Actually, that's the best idea I've heard all day," he said. "Plus, Ms. Vartexia should be waking up right about now."

"Thank goodness she wasn't here," said Emmie. "She'd have had a double heart attack."

As the class began walking back to the Shuttletube, escorted by what looked like a hundred Omega-bots, John noticed a fleck of red in the mud. He bent to pick it up.

"What's that?" asked Kaal, leaning over his shoulder for a better look.

"Piece of the Goran's claw I broke off," John told him, turning it between his fingers. "It didn't make it back into the stasis cube."

"Nice souvenir."

"Exactly what I was thinking." John tucked it into his pocket.

* * *

"Goodness me!" screeched Ms. Vartexia, as she opened her eyes to see the entire class peering at her. "What time is it? Did I miss breakfast?"

"I'm afraid so," said Bareon cheerfully. "Lunch, too."

The Hyperspace History teacher looked aghast. "You mean I've been asleep half the day?" she blurted. "How on Elvar did that happen? Where have you all been? Why did no one wake me? What are those Omega-bots doing here?"

"One question at a time," replied Bareon soothingly. "Everyone is fine. We tried to wake you but you must have eaten too much Elvian spaghetti last night."

Hiding at the back of the group with Kaal and Emmie, so that the teacher couldn't see their torn, mud-stained clothing, John grinned. Bareon had cleverly avoided Ms. Vartexia's questions about the Omega-bots by reminding her of her own mistake.

He watched as the Elvian's face turned green.

"Too much spaghetti? Oh no, it can't have been that. I only had —"

"Four bowls," Queenlin supplied.

Ms. Vartexia flushed an even deeper green.

That's an Elvian blush, John guessed.

"I don't know what came over me. Well, perhaps we should all head back to Hyperspace High before something awful happens. I am sorry, you must have had a terribly boring morning."

"Yes, Ms. Vartexia," the class chorused.

CHAPTER 15

One by one, the Privateers swept into space. Yesterday seemed a million years ago, as did the nerves John had suffered over his takeoff and landing. Now, he executed a perfect exit from the planet's atmosphere without thinking about it. His mind was on something else. As the small spaceships cleared the web of security satellites orbiting Archivus Major, he activated a communications channel to Kaal and Emmie's ships.

"I can't stop thinking there is something really weird about Graximus Greyfore," he said abruptly.

"You said something about him planning the whole thing earlier," Emmie answered. "I wasn't really listening, though. Sorry, I was scared out of my mind at the time."

"I was wondering about it, too," said Kaal. "The Comet Creative looked like a 4-D camera on the outside but there was no image capture technology inside at all."

"Why would the curator want to unfreeze a whole battle, though?" Emmie asked. "I mean, did you see what that Subo's laser did to the Omega-bot? It wouldn't have taken long for either army to break through the force field and then —"

All three of them were quiet for a moment, thinking about what might have happened if the warring Goran and Subo had been able to break free.

"It *might* have been a mistake," said Kaal eventually. "These things happen. Maybe he's like Ms. Vartexia. Perhaps he gave Emmie the wrong device by accident."

"No, I'm certain he planned it," said John firmly. "He told Emmie she would get extra credit, but how could he make a promise like that if it was a secret from Ms. Vartexia and Lorem? Plus, he was very keen to recommend the Elvian spaghetti to Ms. Vartexia."

"*And* he told Mordant that the Vaporball Championship was on a planet close to Archivus Major," Kaal said thoughtfully.

"So, everything that went wrong can be traced back to Graximus Greyfore," said John. "But Emmie's right: *why*? Why would the curator try to wreck his most famous exhibit?"

"Unless Graximus Greyfore isn't everything he seems," said Kaal.

Silence descended again. Stars and planets swept by, but this time none of them bothered to look. They were all lost in their own thoughts, as their ships powered through space.

After a minute had passed, Emmie sighed. "Do you think this means I *won't* get extra credit?"

CHAPTER 16

"So, I guess we should tell Ms. Vartexia what *really* happened on Archivus Major before we get back," said John.

As the words left his mouth, a light flashed on the Privateer's display skin.

"Emergency distress beacon detected at coordinates eighty-four point twelve point eight two zero," the computer announced. "A point-three FTL Jet. Identity codes confirm it is an Archivus Major craft. Instructions?"

Instantly, John forgot about Graximus Greyfore and the Comet Creative. He didn't hesitate. During Space Flight Theory class, Sergeant Jegger had drummed emergency procedures into his students. Every pilot knew that a ship in trouble should be approached with extreme caution.

Putting aside all other thoughts, John immediately began the procedures Jegger had taught. "Scan for weapons, engine efficiency, and signs of damage," he said automatically. "Establish a communication channel, code one, and prepare to intercept. Magnify."

An image of a clunky-looking white spaceship with Archivus Major markings appeared on the screen. "Intercept course plotted," said the computer. "No weapons. Engines and communication systems inoperative. Distress call level alpha."

Opening a new channel, John said, "Ms. Vartexia, I'm receiving a distress call. A ship from Archivus Major."

"We are all picking up the same signal," Ms. Vartexia replied.

Her voice sounded clipped and efficient, but beneath, John heard a quiver of worry. He knew what was causing it. Without communications, there was no way of knowing what had happened aboard the distressed ship. Whatever it was might put the students in danger. But every pilot in the galaxy knew that a distress beacon could not be ignored. Seriously injured beings might be on board.

Ms. Vartexia appeared to reach a decision. Sounding more sure of herself, she began to give orders: "John Riley, you are two minutes closer than the next ship. Proceed to the coordinates and lock onto the craft with your tractor beam.

Take it directly to Hyperspace High. The rest of us will take formation beta twelve around you and escort you in. All craft maintain a continuous scan. Keep communication channels open. At the slightest sign of unusual activity, every ship is to leave the vicinity of the damaged vessel immediately. Clear?"

"Yes, Ms. Vartexia."

Switching navigation to manual, John increased his speed and turned away on a new heading. Within a few minutes, he no longer needed the magnified image of the crippled ship. It was dead ahead: a slowly spinning spaceship larger than the Privateer. It reminded John of a large camper van.

Cutting speed, he took his ship close. There was no sign of life and no clue to what had happened inside. Carefully, he turned the Privateer and brought it to a complete stop.

"Computer: tractor the distressed ship on my mark. *Go.*"

"Tractor beam engaged."

John looked over his shoulder. The Archivus Major ship had stopped spinning. It was held fast by a glowing white energy field.

"Maintain constant scan and set course for Hyperspace High. Maximum speed."

"Affirmative."

Ms. Vartexia and the rest of the class brought their ships into tight formation around him. All communication channels stayed open but there was a tense silence as John pulled the mysterious ship through space.

* * *

"Approaching Hyperspace High," the computer reported.

Ahead was the elegant sweep of Hyperspace High, blazing with light. With a slight shock, John realized how happy and relieved he was to see the colossal ship: it was almost like coming home. But the feeling faded quickly, replaced instead by alarm.

Soon he would have to land the Privateer, and he would have to do so with another ship in tow. He gulped nervously.

Alarm swiftly started turning to panic as he neared Hyperspace High. The open bay doors looked like the eye of a needle. Far too small to get a spaceship through.

Sergeant Jegger's voice came through the intercom. As if he was reading John's mind, the flight instructor said, "You're going to be fine, cadet. I'll talk you through the approach. On my command, cut your speed. . . . "

Following Jegger's instructions closely, John

brought the Privateer around for a run into Hyperspace High's main hangar.

Gritting his teeth, he flew dead center through the bay door, checking over his shoulder to make sure that the Archivus Major ship was still behind him.

Landing two ships was tricky. As the little Privateer dragged the larger aircraft behind it, John felt like he was trying to pilot a whale. Bumping to the ground, John felt the distressed ship smack into the deck behind him.

"Not perfect, but good enough. Well done, cadet," said Jegger. "Stand by for compression."

Once the other students had also landed their ships, the massive bay door slid shut. As the hangar deck filled with air, several doors opened at once.

The headmaster walked through one, Jegger at his side, both looking stern. A medical team came through another, while Examiners swarmed in from the rest. John had never seen so many Examiners in one place. Like the Omega-bots on Archivus Major, the robots immediately formed a protective ring around the mysterious ship.

John climbed out of his Privateer without taking his eyes off the craft he had just towed from deep space.

"Keep back," said Lorem, as John walked toward it. He nodded at the headmaster and stepped back a pace or two. Kaal and Emmie fell in behind him, both gazing at the Archivus Major ship.

Its door opened with a hiss.

A short figure staggered onto the deck. "Help. P-p-p-please *help*!" yelled Graximus Greyfore, reaching his stubby hands toward the headmaster. "I have been —"

"It was him!" John shouted. Unable to contain himself, he ran toward the curator. "He used us to sabotage the Goran-Subo battlefield."

"He nearly got us all killed!" shouted Kaal, rushing forward to join his friend.

"Why did you give me the Comet Creative?" demanded Emmie. "Why did you want to free the Subo and Goran warriors?"

"What?" squealed Ms. Vartexia. "What is everyone talking about?"

"John Riley, explain," said Lorem quickly.

"Three days ago in the lecture hall, Greyfore gave Emmie a camera — he called it the Comet Creative — and told Emmie to take photos of the Goran-Subo battlefield," replied John. "But when she used it, the stasis cube melted and the Goran and Subo immediately began fighting again."

Surrounded by Examiners, Greyfore looked

around in confusion. The whole class began talking, all trying to tell the story at once.

The headmaster clapped his hands. "Silence," he said in a voice that could not be disobeyed. "Continue, John."

John took a deep breath. Suddenly everything was becoming clear. "Headmaster," he said. "When Graximus Greyfore visited Hyperspace High, he requested the Holo-registrations so that you would have to leave the room. While you were gone, he somehow made people do what he wanted in order for the Goran and Subo to be freed from stasis."

"But I don't understand. That couldn't have happened. I just fell asleep for a little while," said Ms. Vartexia, sounding faint.

"It's all true," said John firmly. "Ask him," he said, pointing at the curator again.

"Perhaps we *should* hear what Graximus

Greyfore has to say." Turning to the curator, the headmaster lifted an eyebrow. "Well, Greyfore?" she said.

"I d-didn't do a-anything," stammered the little alien.

"You deliberately told me to eat the Elvian spaghetti at Optical Orbit, knowing it might keep me unconscious for hours," said Ms. Vartexia in a thoughtful voice. "Now that I think about it, that *was* strange. I don't particularly like Elvian spaghetti, but it was as if I couldn't see anything else on the menu. Once I started eating it, I just couldn't stop."

"And you made sure that Mordant Talliver knew the Vaporball Championship was being held nearby," added Kaal.

Lorem's purple eyes widened. "Of course, that meant I would have to go after him, leaving the rest of the students unprotected."

Pausing for a moment, Lorem gave Graximus Greyfore a chilly stare. "With myself and Ms. Vartexia unable to help, you made sure that once the Goran and Subo broke free from stasis, the class would be caught up in the battle. They would be killed, leaving no survivors to point the finger at you. Fortunately, it seems that my students were braver and more resourceful than you could have imagined. But how did you do it, Greyfore? And another, even more important question: why?"

At last the curator found his voice. "P-please listen," he choked. "It-it wasn't m-me."

The shouting began again. Lorem held up his hand, a strange look on his face. "Go on," he said. "I could sense that *something* was going to happen on Archivus Major, but my visions of the future are sometimes . . . unclear."

"It w-w-wasn't me," Graximus Greyfore

insisted, his voice sounding a little steadier. "None of it."

The curator took a deep breath. "I was on my way to Hyperspace High when my ship was hijacked by a Subo craft. Before I could call for help, a Subo came aboard. He called himself Supretus VI and used a machine he had developed — an Xogram Impersonator — to take a sample of my DNA."

"An Xogram Impersonator," whispered Lorem. "But DNA-modifying technology is forbidden throughout the galaxy."

"Then . . . th-then . . . " Greyfore stuttered to a stop, a look of horror crossing his blotched face.

"And then?" the headmaster prompted.

"And then he turned into *me*. R-r-right in front of my eyes."

"So, you're saying that the Graximus

Greyfore who came here was an impostor?" Lorem looked doubtful.

The curator nodded eagerly. "Yes. Not me at all," he babbled.

"But why? Why go to all that trouble?"

"Supretus is a direct descendant of General Klort. For thirty thousand years his family has seen it as a dishonor that she was denied a victory over the Goran. He wanted to free his ancestor and restart the war. Supretus had a small hypnosis device that fitted into the palm of his hand. He bragged to me that when he touched someone with it, they would do whatever he suggested."

"What a load of nonsense."

A gasp ran around the hangar deck.

Standing in the doorway of the Archivus Major ship was another Graximus Greyfore.

This one was holding his head as if he was

in pain. As everyone watched, he raised a hand and pointed to the first Greyfore, standing before the headmaster.

"It was *him!*" the new Greyfore said in a much deeper voice. "*He* is Supretus. He kidnapped *me.* I was tied up for days but I managed to free myself, disable the ship, and set off the distress beacon. In his rage, he knocked me unconscious."

The first Greyfore stamped his foot in fury. "*L-l-liar!*" he screamed. "You imprisoned me in my own sh-ship while you impersonated me at H-hyperspace High! I don't know h-h-how much longer I could have m-m-managed if no one had answered my distress b-beacon."

"*You* are the liar. If I hadn't stopped you —"

"Enough," commanded Lorem, holding up his hand. "There is an easy way to settle this. Examiners."

"Wait —"

The second Greyfore's shout was silenced as Examiners moved forward. Green light flickered. Both curators were immediately held fast in a force field.

Red beams scanned the two short aliens.

"DNA scan complete. Identified. Graximus Greyfore of planet Dorfius t-Char. Head Curator of Archivus Major," droned one of the white robots.

"Unidentified Subo. DNA modified. Reverting," droned another.

John stared. Around him, students took a step back. Ms. Vartexia yelped in shock.

Where the second Greyfore had been standing was suddenly a Subo. Surrounded by a green haze, it could not move but still looked as fearsome as its ancient cousins had on Archivus Major. Its mouth, lined with sharp teeth, was open wide and its laser-horn was lowered, ready to fire a deadly blast.

A green light flashed. The Subo roared in frustrated rage. "Suboran should have won the war!" he raged in a deep voice. "Klort was robbed of victory. The Subo are the rightful rulers of the galaxy."

"Enough of this madness," said Lorem quietly.

A green light flickered again. The Subo was silenced.

"Intergalactic code violation," droned one of the Examiners. "Supretus VI, you impersonated Graximus Greyfore to start a war. You placed Hyperspace High students' lives in danger. Punishment: expulsion."

John remembered the same punishment had been given to him upon his arrival at Hyperspace High.

He also remembered what happened next.

"Proceed to airlock three."

A door opened. The Examiners' force field effortlessly lifted the Subo from the ground. The creature floated across the deck and disappeared inside the airlock.

"Expulsion code eight five six three," droned the Examiner.

"Decompression in five seconds," replied a deeper voice. "Four . . . three . . . two . . . one."

The last time John had heard these words, it had been him in the airlock. Then, Lorem had intervened at the last second. Now, the headmaster stood perfectly still, his face stony.

Underneath the calm, he's angry, John thought. *Absolutely furious.*

Horrified and fascinated at the same time, John watched through the airlock's small window. He heard a faint hiss, followed by a rushing sound as the oxygen in the airlock was snatched out into space.

With it went the screaming Subo, its scream dying as it disappeared into the void.

CHAPTER 17

"O-oh m-my . . . this is-is-is a-awful. T-truly awful."

With effort, John tore his gaze from the little window of black space he could see through the airlock door.

Graximus Greyfore was shaking, tears of black liquid running down his face. "I-I am s-so glad that your students escaped Archivus Major. B-but this is s-still a disaster."

"Calm yourself, Graximus," said Lorem

gently, bending to lay a hand on the small alien's shoulder.

Greyfore shook the headmaster's hand off. "How can I possibly calm myself?" he wailed loudly. "The Subo and Goran will be r-ripping Archivus Major apart by now. The Omega-bots will not be able to stop them. The greatest museum c-collection ever seen will be g-g-gone. The work of fifty thousand years! Destroyed! W-we must be grateful that your students survived, but —"

"But nothing," said John. "The plan failed."

"F-failed?" Greyfore looked up, hope in his eyes.

John stepped forward. "Yes," he said. "Luckily Kaal is an expert with technology. He managed to reverse the process. The battlefield is just how it was when we arrived. Everything on Archivus Major is fine."

"It's s-s-safe? The planet is safe?" Greyfore seemed unable to believe it for a few moments. Then he beamed at the students. "Oh, but that is *wonderful*. Th-thank you. Thank you from the bottom of my third stomach."

"You're welcome."

While Greyfore spoke, the headmaster looked around, watching as the students exchanged looks that told him John had skimmed over a lot of the story. Now he cleared his throat.

"Excuse me," Lorem said. "As I only arrived back from Plarz with Mordant Talliver a few moments ago —"

"I'm terribly sorry to interrupt, Headmaster," Ms. Vartexia cut in. "Really I am. But would someone please tell me what happened on Archivus Major?"

"Exactly what I was going to say, Ms. Vartexia," echoed Lorem. "I understand that

Supretus gave a device to Emmie Tarz that would dissolve the battleground stasis cube, but *how did you manage to stop the warriors escaping?*"

Feeling everyone looking at him, John blushed and shuffled. "Um," he started. "Like I said, it was Kaal. He fixed it."

"The whole story, please, John. Start at the beginning."

With many interruptions from the rest of the class, John finished the tale. At the end, Lorem looked as calm as ever. Only his voice betrayed how much the story had affected him: how concerned he was that the class had been in such terrible danger.

"Thank you, John," he said quietly. "And thank you, too, Kaal and Emmie. You may never know what a great service you have done for the galaxy. I shudder to think what might have happened if you had not managed to put the Subo and Goran back into the stasis cube. Very likely the war would have spread, once again, across the galaxy. You may have saved countless lives and civilizations."

The headmaster paused, then continued sorrowfully. "I made an error. I knew that something important would happen on Archivus Major, but in my visions I saw only that Hyperspace High pupils would be involved. I failed to see that 'Greyfore' was not who he appeared to be." He shook his head. "It is fortunate that my error did not have fatal consequences."

"Headmaster, I d-d-don't know how I can ever repay your students," the real Greyfore cut in. "But could I just say that any visitors from Hyperspace High will always be welcome on Archivus Major. The m-m-museum is at your disposal."

"Thank you, Graximus. I think our students should remain on-board for some time, though. Whenever they leave the ship, they seem to become involved in a life-or-death adventure! It may be some time before I allow them to leave my sight again."

The class groaned.

"Can't we go back?" Bareon said. "I got stuck looking after Ms. Vartexia all day and I *really* wanted to visit the Gormib the Reaper exhibition." Bareon caught a sharp glance from the blue-skinned teacher. "Not that looking after Ms. Vartexia was a problem," he muttered.

"Plus the first day, all we got to see was moss and rocks and boring paintings," said Queenlin.

The headmaster clapped his hands together, his cheerful smile restored. "The very least I can do is award the entire class extra credit." He winked at Emmie.

Emmie punched the air. "*Yesssssss*," she hissed.

"What about Mordant?" Lishtig interrupted.

"I found Mordant on Plarz," Lorem said gravely. "At the moment he is confined to his dormitory with an Examiner outside the door. I was planning to expel him, but this information sheds new light on the matter. Since his actions were influenced by Supretus, I see no reason why he should be punished. In fact, I will order a special screening of the Vaporball Championship highlights in the 4-D cinema. All of you are welcome to join him there."

The headmaster raised his voice, as the class began asking more questions. "No classes for the rest of the day, and perhaps a day off tomorrow would also be in order," he announced, to further cheers. "Now, you should all get back to your rooms and get some rest." As the class filed toward the TravelTube, with only Greyfore and the teachers remaining behind, Lorem stopped John, Emmie, and Kaal. "Once again, it seems I owe the three of you special thanks," he said in a low voice. "Hyperspace High is fortunate to have three such brave students."

"Thanks, sir, but it was nothing, really," John mumbled, embarrassed.

Kaal shrugged. "It was exciting in an almost-getting-killed sort of way."

"And totally worth it for the extra credit," Emmie said, grinning.

"There is one last thing," the headmaster continued, holding out his hand. "I will take the Comet Creative, please. It sounds like for all his crimes, Supretus was something of a genius with technology. Perhaps the scholars of Kerallin can find a more peaceful purpose for the device."

Graximus Greyfore leaned in as Lorem took the Comet Creative from Kaal's hand. "Such a small thing," he murmured. "Yet with the potential to cause such an enormous amount of d-d-damage."

"Indeed, Graximus," the headmaster replied. "Don't worry, we shall keep it very safe."

"Now I-I-I must g-get going," said Greyfore. "I want to check the b-b-battlefield exhibit thoroughly. In the meantime, please accept my thanks once again. If there is anything else I can do to repay any of you, please, please do not hesitate to let me know."

"Actually," said Kaal, as the curator turned to go. "There is something. My dad's been longing to visit Archivus Major for years, but the waiting list —"

Greyfore waved a stubby hand. "For your father, there is n-n-no waiting list. He will have an invitation as s-s-soon as I arrive back. Will a week be long enough for h-h-him? No, better make it two. And every night the b-b-best dinner that Optical Orbit can provide." With a final wave, he disappeared into his ship.

"Now, I know that Mr. Riley here dislikes sleeping, except in class," said the headmaster with a smile, "so I won't tell you to go and rest. But go and relax at least. Try not to get in any trouble."

CHAPTER 18

"I'm starving," said Kaal, as they walked along a corridor toward the dormitories. "Anyone want to take a trip to the Center? Maybe we could get into Seefood while the rest of the school is still in class."

Emmie looked at him as if he were crazy. "*Hello,*" she said. "I'm covered in filth. It's going to take me a day at least to get all the mud out of my hair. There is no way I am going out in public."

"Nah, you look fine," Kaal said. "John looks way worse."

"Yeah, well some of us spent half the day face down in the mud, not flitting around the sky," said John quickly, shocked at the idea of going back to the eyeball restaurant. Silently, he thanked his stars that Emmie had given him an excuse. "A bath's a really good idea. I mean, look at me." He brushed his muddy SecondSkin suit, frowning as his hand passed over a bump in the pocket. Reaching in, he picked out the Goran claw tip. "Oh, I'd forgotten about this," he said, turning it over in his hand. It was about the size of an arrowhead and deep red.

"Hey, you're the only person in the universe to ever take a piece of an Archivus Major exhibit off the planet," Kaal told him. "It's strictly forbidden. You're lucky an Omega-bot didn't catch you."

"*Lucky?*" said John. He laughed, and then added, "I guess I am. Lucky to have such great friends. If it wasn't for you two, I'd be dead by now."

Emmie rolled her eyes. "You're not going to make a big deal out of it, are you?" she asked. "I mean, we could both say the same about *you* and if we all start, it'll end up with hugging and, to be honest, you're *both* dirty and smelly. I really don't want to be hugging either of you right now."

Kaal and John grinned. "Aww, come on, Emmie. Give me a hug," the big Derrilian said. He chuckled.

"Oh, *all right*," she said, and laughed back, flinging her arms around him. "As you did save my life. *Again*. You, too, John," she added, throwing her arms around him, too.

"Umm, thanks. You were pretty cool, too,"

John said, blushing as Emmie squeezed him tight. "Good throwing arm."

"Ugh, now I *really* need a bath," Emmie answered, breaking her hug and looking down at the extra dirt that had transferred to her from John. Smiling once more over her shoulder, Emmie disappeared into her room.

* * *

Half an hour later, John was sitting in his bed pod, absentmindedly turning the Goran claw tip over in his hand while Zepp connected to Earth's internet. By now, he was clean, his still-wet hair slicked back from his head, skin slightly pink from the heat of the bathwater.

"Hello, dear," said his mother suddenly.

John looked up to see his mom and dad smiling at him from the ThinScreen.

"Good grief, our son's been taken by aliens," his dad exclaimed.

John froze. *How could he know? How could he possibly know?*

"And they've managed to clean him! Look how shiny he is. Their technology must be far more advanced than ours."

John felt his shoulders relax. "Hi, Dad," he replied. "Just got out of the shower. Me and Carl were playing around outside, tossing the ball around. Got a little muddy."

"How was the museum trip?" his mother asked.

"It was okay. Lots of old paintings and rocks and stuff like that."

"What's that you're holding?" his dad asked, suddenly, leaning in as if he could peer through the webcam.

John looked at his hand. His heart began to

pound. He'd forgotten to put the Goran claw back in his pocket.

Oh rats.

"Um," he said, his mind blank. "It's an, um . . . uhh . . . " A flash of inspiration hit him. "It's from cooking class — you know, the 'frying' lessons," he babbled, holding up the piece of alien claw. "We made lobster. I saved a piece of claw."

His mother and father looked shocked. "You cooked *lobster* in your cooking class?" his mom said. "*Lobster?*"

John nodded.

"Wow, that school really *is* amazing," whispered his mom.

"Yeah, it's out of this world," said John with a grin.